G R JORDAN

The Disappearance of Russell Hadleigh

A Patrick Smythe Mystery Thriller

First published by Carpetless Publishing 2020

First edition

ISBN: 978-1-912153-94-7

This book was professionally typeset on Reedsy.
Find out more at reedsy.com

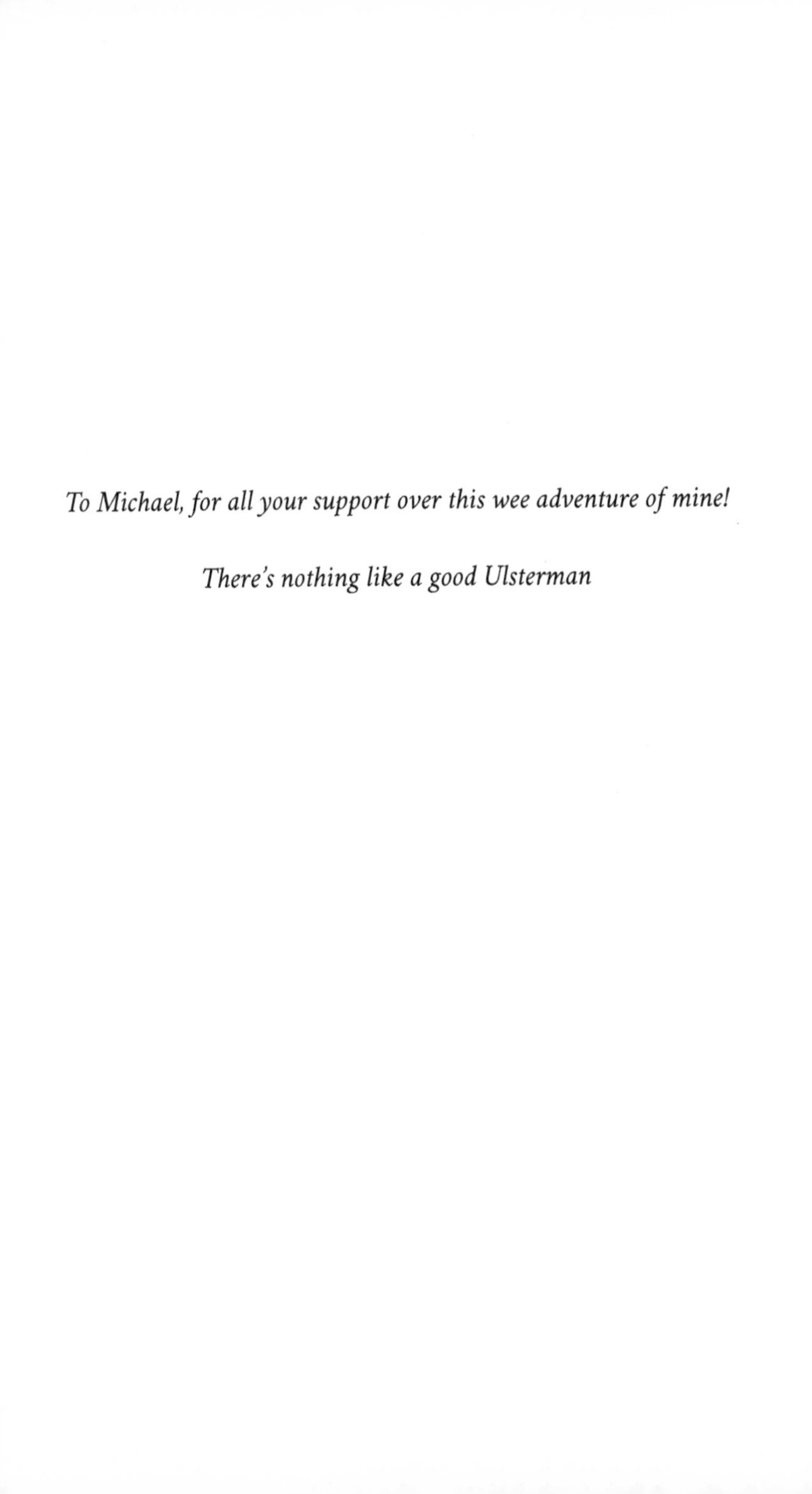

To Michael, for all your support over this wee adventure of mine!

There's nothing like a good Ulsterman

Contents

Foreword

This story is set across the varying landscapes of Scotland's west coast. Although set amongst known towns and lochs, note that all persons and specific places are fictional and not to be confused with actual buildings and structures that exist and which have been used as an inspirational canvas on which to tell a completely fictional story.

Chapter 1

I'm currently sitting in a swimming pool, my single arm resting on the side and very aware that I'm being watched. This happens sometimes. As I have only the one arm, my swimming action is somewhat different to other people. A lot of it comes from the legs. It took a bit of getting used to, but in all honesty, it's now one of my great pleasures to swim. But with my slightly unusual action come a lot of stares and yes, it's rude, but that's people. When they haven't seen something before, they just look and it's to be expected. So, I don't get worried. But now I'm being stared at by a blonde-haired woman of around forty years of age. She also seems not to be shocked, or in some way surprised, about my lack of an arm, but rather, she seems keen on me.

I'd better explain. My name's Patrick Smythe and I investigate things. Well, I more look into things for people. Sometimes, I do this legally. Other times, I bend the law occasionally, but I am one of the good guys. Honest, I am. I used to be a police officer until the day it happened. When you come from Northern Ireland, everybody wants to talk to you about the Troubles, but to be honest, it's the last thing I want to talk about because that's where I lost my arm.

But that's enough said about that. Let's focus on the woman

looking at me. She's got long, blonde hair done up attractively and she's not putting it into the water, so I reckon she spent some time on it. From what I can see, she's got shapely shoulders, but the rest of her is out of view under the water. I don't want her to know I've seen her, so I continue to swim up and down for the best part of half an hour. All the while she sits at the side of the pool, watching.

That, in and of itself, is unusual. If you're looking for someone or if you're trying to catch their eye, rarely do you just sit there and stare. You might move up and down, surreptitiously looking out of the corner of your eye or even adjust your position for a better view. But she's simply looking at me. When I finish my lengths, I climb out of the pool and stand in the showers, rinsing myself down. As quick as a flash she's moving towards me, having climbed off the pool edge. She's wearing a blue bikini and, truthfully, she is attractive, but when I'm being stared at by a woman whom I don't know and who is looking at me with an intensity that frankly scares me, I try to see past what curves or not she may have.

The bikini looks brand new. It doesn't have any of the fade that comes from long-term swimming in a chlorine pool. Unlike my trunks, which quite frankly look like they've had a load of whitewash slapped across them, so jaded are the colours. The woman steps into the shower beside me and starts rinsing herself down. I think she's trying to be provocative, but she doesn't know how, and she simply looks like someone trying to shower with soap, cleaning herself without any sense. This is leaving me a little bit bemused, but as I turn to go away, she speaks in a harsh tone. The voice is husky and it's doing a lot more for me than the bikini did.

'Will you take a walk with me into the jacuzzi?' she says.

As I said before, I'm not used to this, and I want to know her motives. So, I turn around casually and say, 'How much do you charge?' I want to know the cost rather than wake up in the morning to a large bill.

Most women would be horrified at that statement. I would expect a slap, maybe even a knee into my crotch, but she doesn't blink an eye.

'Come with me. I need to talk to you.' And with that, she steps across me, deliberately bumping into me before making her way to the health suite.

I'm slightly annoyed at this as I deliberately picked this swimming pool so people would not bother me. I'm being forced to stay on land for a couple of days due to the boat I live on—*Craigantlet*—getting its bottom scrubbed. One of the things about living on a boat every day of the year is that from time to time you do need to make sure that it's sea-worthy; otherwise, you end up in the drink, as does your house. I do a lot of travelling up the west coast of Scotland and back across to Northern Ireland, but a sailor is only ever as good as his boat. And if the boat gets a hole, you're going in with it, so I spend the money and I look after my boat. Today, it's getting its bottom wiped, all the accumulated debris scraped off. So, I left the harbour, grabbed a taxi, and asked the driver to take me to a gym, one with a swimming pool, somewhere nice that I could be left alone and enjoy the pleasures of a light workout. He brought me here. It's a private sports club, but you can pay for day membership. The cost is exorbitant, but I'm treating myself, and now I've got a woman who wants to take me into a jacuzzi.

As I said before, I'm an investigator, working here and there to find out the real story. So, trust me when I say that this woman's insistence is what's driving me into that jacuzzi. It's not her figure. You can believe me if you want. Entirely up to you.

When I walk through the door into the health suite, I notice the two spa pools and in one an elderly couple are enjoying the bubbles, while my friend has made for an entirely separate one. She's sitting on the side, not yet immersing herself within the agitated water and I guess that's just to make sure that I step in. She's trying to pout, trying to encourage but she's misread me. I need to hear more of her story. She needs to tell me why she's hunting me down. Beyond that, it's a pleasant view but I don't walk openly into places until I know what they are. That may sound a little harsh, but it's kept me alive.

I walk past her and slip into the jacuzzi feeling the warmth from the bubbles, which is not the best thing after completing half an hour's swimming. A long drink of water and resting up is what I need before using any of these types of devices, but as she slips into the jacuzzi beside me, I forget about this and try to concentrate on what the woman's about to say.

'You're a hard man to get hold of, Mr Smythe.'

'Really?' I say. 'Just in a professional capacity or to get hold of to take out to dinner? If you want dinner, it's fine, but you're buying.'

'My husband is dead, Mr Smythe.' This is not something that you normally open with if you wish to chat someone up, so I'm assuming this is going to take an investigative bent. She looks around her and then satisfied no one else seems to be listening, she moves closer to me. I can feel her thigh touching mine. She leans back, tilts her neck to the side and talks directly into my ear. For my part, I sit looking forward as if this is the most normal thing in the world.

'As I said, Mr Smythe, my husband is dead.'

'And if we don't want to sound like some bad spy movie,' I say, 'call me Paddy. And your name is?'

'Alison,' she says. 'Alison Hadleigh.'

'Well, Alison, as much as I appreciate taking me to a jacuzzi, state your business because now I'm on downtime. I've paid a bloody fortune to be in this place and I want to make proper use of it.'

'Like I said, my husband is dead.' With that, I feel a hand resting on my good shoulder. She continues to lean over whispering huskily into my ear. 'He disappeared two days ago, but prior to that, he seemed strange and worried. It was like he was setting things in order as he was bothered about something. He went off for a golf match at the local club, Royal Cairns. It's about twenty miles from here, but he never came home. Sometimes my husband disappears, but he always lets me know where he's going or, at least, he always contacts me to say he's okay. I never ask too much. I don't need to ask too much, but he hasn't contacted me, and he didn't say he'd be away. So, something is wrong, and I firmly believe him to be dead.'

I find this all interesting, but at the moment it means nothing to me. 'Why don't you go to the police?' I ask her. 'They do missing persons and they're free.'

'I don't want to go to the police, Paddy, because they might dig up things that I don't want to be found out. They may also dig up things that cause people to run. They may end up scaring away the people I want brought to task.'

'So why do you come to me?' I say, looking as innocent as anything. 'I'm a one-armed man with a boat that's getting its bottom wiped. What can I do for you?'

'I've been told you're the best, especially when it comes to working behind the scenes.'

'I wouldn't say that. I'm not the best, but the others are dead. Some of them were better than me.'

'Are you interested, Paddy?'

'Interest me with some money.'

'Name your fee. It's not a problem.' This is the kind of talk I like. People who hand you blank cheques. That's always good, but instead of simply grabbing hold of it, I want to see exactly how involved she is in this.

'No, I'm not interested. I don't need to be.' There's a sudden clutch on my arm. Her other hand rolls over to my thigh and she slides herself close into me.

'Please, Mr Smythe, please. I'm afraid if they killed him, they may come for me. My husband was what my husband was, but I don't want to be dead as well. I need protection, I need to know who did this, and I need to know if I need to run.'

'You seem to be talking about a lot of heat. I'm not sure I can be bothered with that at this time.' She rolls over and starts trying to kiss me. I push her back. 'There's no need for that.' But she's shaking now. It's a bubbling hot pool and she's shaking.

'Tell me what you want,' she says. 'Anything.' She's almost pleading with me now. I can see tears beginning in her eyes. The old couple are looking over and probably think they're watching some episode of EastEnders. Inside, part of me laughs, which is probably not a great thing considering I have a very scared woman almost crying in my face, but I tend to see the humour in everything.

'This is not the place to talk,' I say. 'Let's go somewhere else, quiet, private, and out in the open. Do you have a car with you?' She nods. 'Okay, you get out first and go and get changed. When you see me come out of the building, drive up with the car and I'll get in.'

She leans over and whispers a thank you in my ear. 'They said you were the best. I need you to be the best.' Her hands run across my chest before she steps out of the small pool and walks across the wet floor towards the main showers. Yes, I am a man and I did watch her go, but inside my head there's something nagging at me. Why is she so scared? And if she's that scared, why hasn't she just run? What's keeping her? Is it simply the money? Is she that shallow? And how does she really feel about her husband? The only way to find out is to get out of this pool and so I climb out and have a quick shower before changing into my jeans, tee-shirt and jacket. Walking out early on my expensive membership, I see her pull up in a red Porsche. I know this because as she pulls up just beyond me, it says Porsche on the rear. I'm not a great car man, but this one looks classy. Older, not a new model. Maybe if I were unkind, I would say it suited her personality too. Stepping into the car, I see her sitting there, one hand on the wheel, dressed in a white blouse and trousers.

'Thank you for coming along, Mr Smythe; for coming to hear what I have to say.'

'I haven't said I'll do anything yet. I'm just coming for a walk. Find us a park, somewhere discreet, somewhere people don't go, and we'll have a chat about your problem?'

With that her eyes light up and I notice how blue they are. Like myself, she may have some miles on the clock, but she's certainly not banned from the showroom yet. And that's what's bothering me. I almost feel like I'm having a pass being made at me even though her husband's just dead, or so she says.

Whenever a woman comes on to me, I always get worried. A lot of them are turned off by my lack of an arm. Yes, it's wrong, but you get used to it. Nobody wants a car with only three wheels. But there's something behind those eyes and I'm not sure I'm going to get the truth out of her, at least not on this walk.

Chapter 2

Alison floors the red Porsche and we drive out of town heading towards Castle Kennedy, but at some point, we make a turn off, and soon we're in a wooded area with some of those tracks people like to follow. She parks up in what seems to be a ridiculously small car park and we step out.

'There's a circular walk here,' she says. 'It should be pretty secluded. I come here sometimes when I'm not feeling the best. I rarely see people.'

I nod my head and then indicate with my hand. 'Where are we going?' She nods towards the track beyond the car.

Alison quickly starts striding and her pace is quite robust. I'm in no way unfit, but when I'm talking or thinking I do like to walk a bit slower, so I feign a bad injury in my leg asking her to ease down a little.

'Let's take it from the top. You say you think your husband has possibly been murdered. Tell me who he is. Tell me all about him and while you're at it, tell me about you.'

She nods. 'My name's Alison Hadleigh. I'm an ex barrister and my husband is Judge Russell Hadleigh. He's a bit of a name in these parts, having sat in some of the major cases around here.'

When she mentions his name, she puts her hand up and runs it through her hair and then ties it up, before letting it go loose again. For a woman who's worried about her husband, she's also paying me plenty of attention. I'm getting little smiles, not worried looks and everything just feels a little funny. I've known people who are panicked before. I've known people try and please me because they're worried, but this isn't that. She feels more like a player and there's something behind it, but I can't grasp what it is.

'It was only two days ago that he left to the golf club. That's the Royal Cairn's golf club, about twenty miles outside of Stranraer. It's a very plush parkland course. You have to be somebody to get in.'

'And is he a keen golfer?'

'Very. He played at least once a week, two to three times if he could get away with it, depending on what other duties he had. He liked mixing it with all the bigwigs, the businessmen, and everyone. If he had time off, that's where he would go.'

'And are you a member?' I ask.

'Like hell I am. I wouldn't be mixing with that lot out there. Halfway up their own backsides.'

'So how did you meet?'

'I worked in the same law court as him. He saw me coming up as a young barrister. After trying several of my cases, he asked me out to dinner. He's quite dashing, Russell, really. He was at least twenty years older than me and I remember at the time being quite flattered and taken aback that he was even interested. I held him in quite high esteem then. We had a couple of years of fun, a couple of years when I thought we were meant for each other and then it kind of died away. We tried to have kids but couldn't. His fault, not mine, and then life slowly went off in two different directions. We shared the same house with plenty of money coming in and we just got on with it.'

'Out here in the sticks?' I ask. 'I mean, it's not exactly a big town.'

'We moved out here for the scenery. We had a second home down in Glasgow before he retired. I've given up the law practice now, happier to just faff about and do what I want. You can get sick of having a go at people every day, standing in a room, driving at them, bringing them to tears. I had enough so I decided to take what was mine.'

'And so, what do you do now? I mean, you're not exactly an old woman.'

This seems to please her, and she smiles at me. 'You start to feel a little old, don't you? I mean, it's not every day I wear a bikini. In fact, it's been five years, at least.'

'Well, I'm honoured then,' I say, trying to butter her up and she takes it, smiling at me, but I may have overcooked it. So I press off on a different tack. 'Where was your husband going that day? I mean specifically. And who was he meeting at the club? What were they going to do?'

'He was off to meet his buddy, John Carson. John's a businessman in the town and Russell played with him a lot. He's sharp on the course apparently, not that I have a clue. He said something about his handicap being under five, if that's any good. I wouldn't know myself. John's retired now, if I remember right. He was a builder.

'John rang me that evening—or rather he rang Russell—but Russell not being in, I told him so and he said to me, 'Russell didn't turn up for the golf.' John had had to play a round on his own. When I said to him that Russell hadn't turned up, John was quite agitated. I don't know. John always seemed quite normal unlike a lot at the club. I don't know if you understand, Mr Smythe, but you can get some right rats up there and when you cross through the good side of the law, it's easy to pick up offers.'

'It's okay. You can call me Paddy. And did your husband pick up offers?'

'I wouldn't say Russell was bent. What I would say is that he was quite happy to align himself if it was legal. He'd take all the dinners going from people as long as he couldn't be held to account for it. As long as it didn't mean having a visit from the boys in blue, Russell was up for it. He enjoyed that and enjoyed mixing with the elite.'

'Did he ever take you there to any of these dinners? Any functions?'

'In the early days he did.' I notice a touch of nostalgia and she turns her head away looking elsewhere as if lost in thought. 'But that was back in the day when he'd like to show me off. I think I was quite a catch for him, but that's what they all did. Most of them had wives that were younger, some five, ten years younger. I was a good twenty younger than Russell but I don't think that's why he picked me, yet that's certainly what it turned into after about five years.' There's a choke in her voice and then regret. 'Maybe that's all I am. Just a trophy wife, but at least I'm a trophy wife with money.'

There's a crunch under our feet. We've walked across some neatly cut branches which have been taken down from trees by our side. This is due to the path narrowing, being enclosed by the overhanging trees and someone has taken up on them to make sure the path is useful and not blocked. I look around me trying to see if anyone's still about, but there's no one. It's just birdsong, the kind you get on those bright mornings. There's a number of different calls. The quick chirp, a long drawn out one, and one that sings like they can go on forever. When I've had the time, I've stopped and listened because it's quite delightful, but I don't have time now, so I prepare myself to ask a few more delicate questions.

'Alison, hope you don't mind me asking this, but I need to know. Are you sleeping around? Have you got anybody on the side?' She looks at me in horror. 'Well, in honesty it's a fair question. Your husband's disappeared. I need to know if he's got any lovers after him.'

'No,' she says, and the tone is firm. 'I don't have anyone else.'

'You said it was five years and then everything went downhill, at least in the close personal relationship side of things. Had anybody in that time?'

'No.' Again, the tone is firm and I'm not sure if I believe her.

'It's okay by me if you did. I'm not here to judge. I'm here to find out what's happened to your husband, so if you have had anything extra marital, just tell me.'

She looks away and then back. 'No,' she says. 'I haven't jumped into bed with anyone and no one has had me, as you put it. I may have flirted occasionally on a night out but no one's got more than a peck on the cheek, so your answer is no, Mr Smythe.'

'Okay, fine. Like I said, it's Paddy. Tell me about the club because I think I'll need to pay a visit. Do you know if that's possible?'

'Well, I know Russell used to take people up. You can't go as a visitor alone. Maybe you need to be signed in. Like I said, I don't bother with the club. That's his world.'

'Have you ever been up at all?'

'About a year ago we went up for wedding anniversary of one of the golfers and his wife. Had to get all dolled up. Bizarre at that age. You see them all sitting there showing off this wife and that.'

'Anyone Russell in particular got on with, or anyone you saw him being close to?'

'Well, Paddy, he's got a lot of friends up there. John's his main one. John's the one he always talks about in any sort of favourable way. The rest of them, it's just scandal or gossip. And they don't keep coming around.'

'What about the people that work at the club? When he was there that evening, did he talk to anybody in particular?'

'There was the girl behind the bar he was very friendly with. Joking friendly. I never got the impression he was doing anything with her, but she seemed to be that sort of person who he would like to tease with, like to flirt with even if it's nothing serious.'

I nod. *We'll see if it's serious,* I think. We continue to walk round and she tells me about the banalities of her life. Russell should have been home but they don't keep plans together. She says it's more like a lodging arrangement now. Although they're both landlords, they have different rooms they sit in in the evening and quite often they don't pass a comment. It's only the golf that he tells her about, though she doesn't know why.

The track is indeed circular and as we come down a small hill, I see the car park where we parked. There's no one there and I invite Alison to get back into the Porsche. Just as I'm stepping round into my side, then I spot a tire track. It hadn't been there when we arrived and it's very close to the Porsche. It could mean nothing. It could mean something. I tell Alison

I've been caught short and to wait in the car. She gives me a disgusted look and I get that, but this is no random need for a pee. This is calculated. I see the tire tracks move off and I believe they disappear though a group of trees and behind a row of bushes. Disappearing into a thicket, and once I'm assured I can't be seen, I step through the other side of the thicket and circle round.

I can see a car, so I keep low moving further round. Keeping a bush between me and its rear-view mirror, I get close and clock the number plate. I sit and wait, hoping the person might get out. It's a man, not that well-built, judging by the fact he doesn't show much beyond the seat. He's got binoculars and his hair is silver. I can't tell if he's young or old, but given the silver hair, he's probably not twenty. And I settle in to wait.

It's about five minutes and then Alison gets out of the Porsche. I can hear her calling to me, asking if I'm all right. It's at this point the man in the car moves. She's obviously gone out of sight and the car door opens and he stands up. He's wearing a charcoal suit, not something you go running around the forest in to try and spy on people. Maybe this was more on the cuff of the moment rather than planned. He's not going to walk round to where she is, so I make my way back to the thicket I entered and come out the other side.

Alison's standing there still shouting after me. 'Sorry, I didn't hear you.'

'Are you all right?' she says. 'You were gone ages.'

'Yeah, I got caught short. Sorry about that. I was making sure it was all put away tidy.' There is a horrific look on her face, quite disgusted, and we walk in silence back to the car. Once inside I tell her what I've seen.

'And you got the number plate?' she asks.

'Yes,' I reply. 'Navy, BMW,' and I recite the number plate to her.

'I think that's John Carson's. Why the hell's he lurking after me?'

'Has he ever looked at you with eyes that say more than just hello? Has he ever been interested in you?'

'No, don't be silly,' she says. 'You keep on banging down this line. I'm not like that.'

'No, but he might be. Just because you haven't dated someone, just because you haven't had an affair, doesn't mean that someone else isn't interested in you.'

'Stop,' she says. 'That's a creepy thought and he's never given me an impression of being a stalker.'

'No? That's good. But why the hell is he watching you?'

'I have a good mind to go and ask him.'

'No, you don't,' I say. 'Start the car and drive off. When we go through the traffic, I'll see if he's still following, but you just drive, okay.' She nods, opens up the Porsche, reverses it, and then drives out back along the small tracks to the main road. Once we're on the main road, I check the rear-view mirror. Sure enough, the car is there, following along behind us. I take over the directions, telling Alison to turn this way, that way, and every time, the BMW follows us. It certainly doesn't look like the tail of an expert. I give a few more instructions and we soon lose him. After we pull over in a car park, she asks me how to contact me. I take a note of her number and I hand her a mobile. It's brand new. It's a thing I have. I tend to keep one on me at all times just in case I contact someone I need to keep in touch with. I tell her it's preloaded with certain numbers and that she can ring me. I make a note of her address.

'Where are you staying?' she asks?

'I'll be in town. One of the hotels.'

'If you want, I can put you up if that's easier for you.'

'That's not really standard practice,' I say. 'It can get a bit awkward if somebody just suddenly turns up. How would you explain me? Who am I? Especially at a time when your husband's missing. If we have to call in the police, what am I doing there?'

'You could stay covertly,' she says. And her hand comes forward grabbing my wrist.

'Why, Alison? Why?'

'Because I'm scared. You said somebody's following me. My husband is missing. I know he was involved in stuff he never talked to me about. I know he put people away who might come after him. I'm scared. If I have you about the house it would just make things easier.'

I sit back in the seat, giving the appearance of mulling it over, but I've made my decision and I'm staying. Not because I'm unprofessional, and not because I have an attraction to her. Although, in fairness, there's going to be a little bit of that in there. I'm also incredibly wary of her. Is she wanting me there to keep tabs on? Is she genuinely scared? There's too much I don't know at the moment and I need to find out, but one thing that strikes me, I will need to return to my boat because I'm going to need my set of golf clubs. Time to get the old swing back in action.

Chapter 3

I'm not one to hang about, so, after I've popped back to Craigantlet and picked up my clubs and a couple of changes of clothing, I drop round to the Hadleigh's residence and Alison shows me to my room. She's dressed in a long skirt and a blouse that must be for my benefit. In fairness it works; that's a most pleasant image. But I've work to do. I tell her I'll be out for most of the afternoon and she asks if she can come along as well, but once I point out the fact that that makes undercover work quite difficult—dragging around the spouse of the missing man—she relents.

I take a taxi from the house and pick up a hire car in town. It's an automatic. Generally, I prefer one that's a manual, but obviously adapted for my single arm. They don't have any of them. So, I have to take the standard automatic and remind myself, don't get involved in any car chases. Approaching the golf club, I see a tree-lined road, the asphalt rising here and there, giving glimpses of the occasional green. A splendid clubhouse stands in the middle, surrounded by practice putting greens, a generous veranda at the back and a car park that's relatively full, giving the fact the day is going south. Rain has begun. And there's certainly a nip in the air for the time of year.

I'm no longer in jeans, but instead wear a smart pair of slacks and a shirt, mainly because a lot of these places frown on you if you look like you're from the rough side of life. I also want to give the impression that I have a bit of money, although that's not strictly true. Entering via the main door, I ask someone where I can talk about membership for the week as I'm visiting. The person's a member himself, called Ian, and he's pleasant enough, pointing me towards the pro shop. It sits neatly at the front of the building and on entry I see the lines of golf shoes, Pringle jumpers and a lot of clubs sitting in racks. A bald-headed man approaches asking if he can help, and I tell him my issue. Here for a week, needing to play some golf. Can he assist with some sort of temporary membership for the week? He nods, asks me to come over, sign a few bits of paper and then announces some figure that I do my best to hide the shock of before handing over my credit card. This is definitely going on the expenses bill for the job.

I ask the man if he's got time to show me around so I know where I'm going, but he says he's in the middle of something, then stops, disappears into the backroom and shouts out. A young woman emerges who must be late teens at best. He announces her as one of the best golfers around and she shakes her head laughing at him, but then he becomes a little bit more formal, calling her Susan. She's got a long shock of red hair, pale white skin, and a very pleasant demeanour about her. She steps forward, shakes my hand, and when I tell her my name, addresses me as Mr Smythe. I tell her to stop being ridiculous, to call me Paddy and she says to call her Susan. It's all very delightful, but what I'm here for is to find out about the club. And so, I ask her if it's possible that she could show me around. Her boss gives her the nod and she disappears with me through the back door of the shop to the clubhouse.

Like most golf clubs, there appears to be vast rooms that aren't used with placards on the wall detailing names of winners of this and winners of that. There's even the odd massive portrait of somebody. He's probably dead now, but he once could hit a ball in a mean fashion around these hallowed greens. Susan takes me through to show me the locker rooms and points out the shower area without going in, just in case any of the men folk are there.

Taking me up to the bar, she points out a girl behind it who also has shocking red hair, and who looks slightly older. That's her sister, named Kirsten. Certainly, the resemblance is quite breath-taking. However, Kirsten is a slightly larger girl, wider in the hips, but nonetheless still pleasant for it. I don't get to speak to her at that point as Susan continues the whirlwind tour and heads off to the restaurant and then takes me down to show me the practice nets and the outside putting greens. And then she turns to me.

'And that's that. That's everything, Paddy. You play much golf?'

I shrug my shoulders. 'You know how it is when you're traveling about. It's not always that easy.'

'So, what's your handicap?'

'Well, I used to play off ten. It's probably a bit higher than that now.'

'If you need a game, I'm happy to give you one,' she says.

'As long as you don't set me up with a ringer,' I reply. 'I'd be delighted to give you a game when it suits.'

'What's wrong with this afternoon?'

'You mean apart from the fact it's pissing down?' I say.

'And what's that got to do with it?' she replies.

'Okay then, let's do it. What time? I mean, it's nearly three o'clock now.'

'If we go at five, we can speed round. If we're tired out, we can cut it short.'

'Sweet, five o'clock. I need to get something to eat then,' I say. 'I'll pop inside up to the bar. What'd you say your sister's name was?'

'Kirsten. Tell her I sent you up. She'll look after you.'

'Thank you, Susan. It's been most entertaining. I'm looking forward to it. But tell me one thing, and I don't mean to be funny about this, but I'm a little bit beyond your age, and I don't want to give the wrong impression here—why do you want to play a round with me.'

She laughs. 'Don't worry, if I'm honest, and I hope this isn't rude, I just want to see how a man with one arm swings a golf club, especially when you tell me you're off ten.'

I laugh, but I look at her eyes and I think there's more than just swinging a golf club involved here. And that's fine. In some ways, it's quite gratifying but who knows where she's coming from? Who knows what her background is? Who knows why she feels the need to flirt and look at a man like me with one arm and twice her age? But it's an entertaining round of golf and good conversation, that's all, and she might be able to tell me a bit as she golfs here a lot.

Taking my leave of Susan, I head up to the bar and introduce myself to Kirsten. She's quite busy at first and gives me a pint before concluding her chat to some of the other golfers. But after about twenty minutes, when she notices I'm still there, she comes over and starts to converse. She's asking what her sister was doing showing me around, and I tell her I'm here for the week, just looking for a game of golf and killing some time.

'So how did you find out about the place?' she asks. 'They're quite reluctant to advertise. Not many people know that you can get a week's membership here. In fact, most people get turned off by it because they never mention it and they never mention to anybody that you can come without a member. You've done quite well for yourself. You see, they had to put those clauses in because certain other places were having a go at them when funds were put into the club and then the club wouldn't open to the public, so now they've opened it. They just haven't done it with a wide door.'

I laugh. 'I bumped into a man who played here. Russell, he's called. Russell Hadleigh. He said he was a judge. We were just doing a bit of business and he mentioned the course was great. I was in the area for the week, so I thought let's come and try it.'

'Judge Hadleigh,' she smirks. 'Now that is one character.'

'Why do you say so? He seemed okay to me.'

'Well, he would, you're male. He has a bit of an eye that tends to rove over a lot of the women that come into this club, not that there's many of us. Not keen at all on the women playing, tolerates the younger women, but the older women, no.'

'I assume you've been the subject of his attention then.'

'I think everyone has. There's nothing shocking about that,' says Kirsten, 'but thank you for the compliment. In fact, he was quite disappointed when he found out I'm going to be engaged.'

'Going to be engaged? You're the first one I've heard say that. Usually you say you're going to be married, not to be engaged.'

'Well, yeah, it's just he's a bit indecisive. I had to tell him what he was going to do.' She laughs and I answer in kind.

'Well, just make sure you don't have to lead him along for everything. That could be quite awkward and disappointing.' She gives me a cheeky smile. It quickly disappears off as she addresses another customer, but as soon as she's free, she comes back.

'Do you know sometimes it gets really dull in here? I sit here and listen to these old husbands whining on. You're quite the breath of fresh air.'

And I spend the next twenty minutes with her flirting gently, not trying to get anywhere with it, not trying to disappear with her, just a gentle flirt. So, we both laugh, and we have a bit of fun. She's doing it to keep herself from being bored. I'm doing it to get somebody on my side, eyes and ears in a place, somebody ready to talk. Some people think that's a bit underhand, but it's not. If people want to talk, people will talk and I like people to talk. It makes things easier. And if I'm truly honest, I live on my own in a boat and I'm a one-armed man, so anytime I can get talking to a pretty woman in a nice relaxed style is pretty good for the ego.

After a while, I order a burger and chips which for such a posh clubhouse seems a bit strange but then again, you're talking about a load of men who play golf. They don't want top cuisine. They want their fried eggs and their chips. They want something that's going to fill them up.

About a quarter to five, I see Kirsten look up. I turn around and her sister, Susan, is coming in the door. She's changed into a skirt, long socks and a smart polo shirt. The skirt goes down to the knees and she looks the image of a young female golfer. Her red hair is now tied up at the back. Coming over to me, she asks if I'm ready and that, if so, she'll see me on the first tee in ten minutes. I nod, finish up quickly, say my farewells to Kirsten, and head off to my car, in order to bring my clubs into the locker room. I have a quick change into decent pair of trousers, a polo shirt of my own and pack a jumper inside the bag just in case it gets cold as we go on into the evening.

The first tee's empty and I can understand why; the day looks pretty grey, although the rain has stopped. But there's a warmth in the air because we're coming into summertime. Susan asks me if I want a proper game, announcing she'll give me a shot a hole if I want. I say, why not, let's put fifty quid on it. She looks a little bit horrified and I'm wondering if she's got fifty quid to her name. But I say to her, 'I won't hold you to it.'

She laughs and says to me, 'I'll give you a peck on the cheek if I lose.' Again, she's flirting like her sister and she doesn't need to.

'Okay, but you're up first. What's your handicap by the way?'

She turns around and smiles. 'They don't give me one.' And I realize I'm probably in for a trouncing.

The first shot off the tee needs to be right down the middle of the fairway. It's a par four. I have to get the ball in the hole in four shots for the uneducated amongst you and the drive, that's the first shot off the tee, is awkward. The hole bends left to right and there's a couple of bunkers that catch you on the left-hand side should you drift out too far. She smacks it right down the middle.

I smack it off to the left and wind up just short of the bunker, but she's impressed. Most people are when they see a one-armed man swing a club. You have to have a lot of strength and the rest you have to time and you certainly can't lash out like a two-armed player can. It really becomes about the rhythm, but then again that's what a two-armed player should be doing anyway. We laugh and joke as we play along and it's only nine holes in that I start to try to ask her some questions about the club. By this point she's very relaxed and I'm thoroughly enjoying my golf. The course is good, the weather's picked up so it's not cold, and I'm playing with a fabulous golfer and yes, she's very good on the eyes too. But she's also exceptionally good for the spirit. Bubbly, lively, and I wonder if there's a bad bone in her body, and that's not normal for me.

'I was telling your sister that it was Judge Hadleigh, Russell Hadleigh, who told me about the club, and I can see why he's pleased with the course. Genuine cracker.'

'Everybody knows Russell Hadleigh, or the Judge as he likes to be called. Certainly, that's what he likes my sister and me to call him.'

'What's he like?' I ask. 'He seemed a nice enough guy to me, but I only just met him on the hoof with business.'

She looks at me sharply. 'Business? Yeah, he's got a lot of business going on. Hope you weren't involved in his funny business.' I look at her and I see how naive she is because if I was someone involved in funny business, it's quite possibly the dumbest comment you could've made.

'No,' I say. 'I wasn't involved in any dodgy business. I just happened to be at a conference he was at and we were talking over a few beers. What do you mean by dodgy business?'

'Maybe I shouldn't say, but you seem alright. He's involved with a few others in this club and a lot of the businesses they run— I don't think they're ethical. You hear conversations on the course or around the clubhouse, and a lot of the time, the things they're talking about, it's putting pressure on people. It's using people. He's heavily in with our club secretary, Angus, Angus Porterfield, and he's a rascal as well. Runs a clothing business, but the stuff he makes is so cheap and knowing some of the workers on this side, they pay some peanuts. We've heard rumours about what they pay them out in the Far East where all the stuff's made. The judge has been, I think, with him on business trips out there. I reckon the judge may even have a stake in it, but I can't be sure.'

'Well, you get a lot of that about places,' I say. 'He seemed a nice enough man to me. Do you ever have any other problems with the Judge?'

'Only the usual. It's one of the things about being a golfer here, being young and female. Some of them look at you like you're some sort of object. They're not nice people like yourself.'

'Have a lot of problems like that?' I ask.

'Yes, I do.' She says. 'And I get a lot of offers to go and play a round.'

I feign a shocked face. 'Play around?'

'No, no, not that,' she says. 'Well, I've had the odd one for that. I meant play a round of golf. If any of them get too frisky on a round, I soon tiptoe around their comments,' she says, making sure I understand. 'They'd have to be far nicer than that, maybe a good man like you,' she says.

I nod. 'Maybe a good man like me and twenty years younger.'

She laughs. 'I don't think youth and age matter.'

'Age does matter,' I tell her. 'It matters to me,' and then I go slightly sullen. I'm thinking about my lonely life and why should it matter? *She looks like she can handle life on a boat. Looks like a lot of fun. A sporting girl who likes her golf, probably lots of walks.* And then I snap back out of it. Sometimes, you get lonely doing this job, but it's no excuse to go off and do something silly.

'Anyway,' I say. 'Playing golf the way you play, you want to be hitting the big tours one day.'

'That's not as easy to get into as you think,' she says. 'And besides, I'm good, but I'm not that good yet. I only took the game up three years ago after my sister started and she wanted somebody else to come and play with her, to keep those annoying men off her back.' Again, we both laugh. The round finishes and I shake hands, having been completely thrashed. I take fifty pounds out of my wallet and hand it to her. She shakes her head.

'I insist, fair and square.'

'In that case,' she says, 'you deserve this.' She reaches forward and gives me a peck on the cheek before stepping back. 'Do you want to go for a drink somewhere?' she says. 'Not up here, somewhere else.'

I'm tempted. I am completely tempted. 'Can I take a rain check?' I say. 'Don't take this the wrong way but I've got somewhere else I have to be tonight and if I'm taking you for a drink, I really need to know why I'm doing it.'

She looks at me, laughs a bit and then goes quite serious. 'You know there's a lot of guys who'd have just snapped at that and just taken me, but you didn't. You're actually worried about me, worried about us. That's quite something. It's very alluring,' and again she steps forward and kisses me on the cheek. 'Take care, Paddy. If you're here for the week, you can find me in the pro shop anytime. It's where I work. It's where I play. Thanks for the game.'

With that she turns and walks off. I stop myself from giving her a lingering look and get back to my car. There's another woman I need to see tonight because I don't think she's been telling me the truth about her husband.

Chapter 4

Because I'm stopping at Alison Hadleigh's, I decide not to drive up in the car and park outside the house. Instead, I leave the car a number of streets away and walk round, choosing to skim past the place first of all, to see if there are any watching eyes. I've put on my prosthetic arm as well, just because it always confuses people when I appear with two arms. When I get spotted or they try to remember me, they see a man with two appendages, not one. It's always a good defence. It's not like I lost it in the meantime.

The street is on one of those impressive avenues with a double road, trees that split either side of it and yet more trees on the edges secluding the houses. These are houses for rich people, people with money, who want their own privacy, and also to be living on a street with a name. The name of this one is Fairbanks Avenue and it's definitely at the posh end of Stranraer.

It's a long and straight street, and as I walk along it, I notice there are a couple of cars parked up. The first of them doesn't have anyone in it. Another has a couple, quite young—possibly the boyfriend dropping off his girlfriend to her house without the parents needing to know. But the third interests me greatly.

It's directly opposite Alison Hadleigh's house and there's

a single man inside, looking over. I casually saunter past, glancing around, trying to catch the features of the guy. I walk away from the street and around the corner. Then I take off my jacket, in what was quite an awkward manoeuvre for me, turn it inside out, and put it back on. I take a hat out of the pocket, place it on my head and hopefully look a vastly different person. This time walking past, I manage to catch a full view of the man as he briefly spins his head round to grab something off the dashboard. It's the same man I saw out in the forest. Mr John Carson. Why is John Carson nosing here? Why is he keeping an eye? Surely all Hadleigh did was miss a golf appointment. There's no reason for him to be here.

I decide it's best if I am not seen entering the house and so go around to the back where another set of large houses are joined onto the rear of Fairbanks Avenue. I walk along, then skip up the drive of one, unfortunately sending off the security light before racing into the hedge rows. Jumping over the back, I walk up to the rear of Alison Hadleigh's house. She has a conservatory and I gently tap on the window.

There's only one light on in the house and I watch someone spark to life, gradually heading towards the conservatory. In a long dressing gown, she enters the room and spies me at the door. Quickly, she makes her way over, unlocks the door before returning inside. I sneak inside, lock the door again, switch the light off and follow her. Once we're out of the conservatory, she turns to me looking rather indignant.

'Where have you been? It's nearly gone eleven.'

'I didn't know I was here for an appointment. You offered me a place to crash. I'm crashing here. I'm sorry if you waited up. You didn't leave any keys, not that that would have been a problem. I only knocked because it's a lot more friendly and stops people getting spooked.'

She looks at me indignantly. 'You're on my payroll.'

'I am indeed on your payroll, but I say how I investigate things. If that's not appropriate to you, I can leave. It's not a problem.'

I see the anger in her face but then it recedes, and she reaches forward taking my hand. When she realizes she's grabbed the prosthetic, she looks a little embarrassed before taking my right hand. 'I almost forgot for a moment,' she says. 'Would you like to go and get changed? Maybe we can have a drink.'

I don't for one minute trust her. Is she trying to plan something with me? Is she generally trying to come on? I know she's up to something, so I simply nod, take myself upstairs before coming down in a pair of slacks and a shirt. She seems somewhat disappointed at my appearance, but I notice that the dressing gown is no longer tied up.

Handing me a glass of wine, she offers me a seat. There's a large sofa sitting in front of a generous fireplace made of marble and on top of it are a number of figurines as well as photographs, probably various parts of the family, certainly some of the judge. She takes a glass of wine, sits down beside me, close enough so our legs are actually touching. Turning sideways and making sure her legs are showing, she puts a hand up to her chin, trying to seem casual and relaxed, but not succeeding. 'So tell me, Paddy, how is our investigation going?'

'Proceeding,' I say, 'but I need some information from you first. When your husband went to play golf, was it simply John Carson he played with?'

She shakes her head. If I'm not mistaken, she's flinging her hair about for my benefit. It's not worth it at the moment. I'm too focused on the case and I need to know names. Now that I've got someone in the club who likes me, I might be able to get a round with some of these people.

'Russell had a number of partners he played with. If you look over there,' she says, pointing towards the mantlepiece, 'towards the far end, bring down that photograph. And the one beside it.' I walk over and pick up the two photographs, bringing them back. Sitting at her side as she takes them from me, I find her moving in close and placing them with one side of the photograph on my knee and the other on hers, meaning we have to draw close to look at them.

'That's his main four-ball. If you notice the businessman—I believe he's also the club secretary. Russell didn't play with him that often, but he did at large events. John was his regular partner, but that man and the man beside him, they'd always get together for the big four-balls.

'He's called Angus Porterfield and he owns some clothing shops, not just here but in different parts of the country. Produces them himself, big in the Scottish market, pretty successful. As far as I know, my husband had some dealings with him. He paid Russell as an advisor at one point, but I'm not sure for what, but I do know that Russell made much money out of it. In fact, a good bit of money. He was still full-time judge at that point and they have been firm friends ever since.

'The man beside Porterfield is a friend of his; I think his name was Lasseter, although my husband always called him Sergei. He does have that Russian look about him, doesn't he? I have no idea where he lives. I'm not sure he's even local to the area, but at the big four-balls, Sergei was always there.'

'And what about the other photograph?' I ask. 'That seems to be a mixed pair. That's your husband and John Carson. Who are the two women?'

'The one with John is his daughter. She always turned up to play. I think that's how he'd first got into playing. They played the mixed only; Russell was never up for playing a round of golf with other women. He used to come in and moan about how the club had suddenly had to take women in. He was a bit late for the revolution. Not what you call a modern man, didn't really believe in the modern woman. We should keep our place. You agree with that?'

I shake my head. 'Absolutely not. I don't want to have a woman with me as you can see but if I did have a woman with whom to share my life, it'd be shared a lot more fairly than that.'

It sounds very egalitarian what I said. Is it honest? It is, actually. Can she tell if it's honest? No, she won't have a clue what I'm thinking and that's the idea. You have to be incredibly careful what you give up.

'You look like a man that's been without a woman for a while. You've got that look in your eye. That hunger. I see men who are like that. They see what they want—they're missing company. Maybe you shouldn't deny yourself that.'

I wave my hand dismissively and look at her. 'I'm working so I deny myself, but back to the point, who's the other woman?'

She seems frustrated. Although sophisticated, the woman is not like Alison. She's brunette and she appears to be about thirty years of age. She's wearing a very trim top, sporting fashionable trainers, all presented with a broad smile. Her hair neatly drapes over her shoulders, disappearing nearly halfway down her back.

'That,' she says, 'is Laura Sutherland. I hate that he still has that photograph of her. Understand she's never to be spoken of in this house.'

Now this is getting interesting. 'Why?' I ask.

'Because I caught her. I caught her and Russell at it in our conservatory of all places. Can you believe that? I came back with the shopping one day. I think he's out, so I walk in quite happily. I start putting things in the kitchen, but I can hear noises. When I step through into this room, I saw the open doors to the conservatory. I find Russell without a top and holding a towel. When I asked him what he was doing, he said he was sunbathing inside. So, I walked through into the conservatory and who do I find hiding behind one of our chairs? Fully starkers, the pair of them in our conservatory at that. Well I threw the little trollop out, and him with her for a couple of days.'

'That is a bit extreme,' I say comforting her. 'But you let him come back.'

'Of course, I let him back. I've never believed Russell would be faithful to me in my life and he's probably had other women, too. But you don't do it on your doorstep when you are married. Yes, I was head over heels. So was he. But that paled quickly. I don't need a divorce; I have his money and I have my money. And at some point, Russell will disappear off. If he wants to divorce me, he can bloody well pay me, but if he's not about—well, this is all mine and I'm quite happy about that.'

I can't believe the audacity of the woman. She's sitting there, thighs on show, telling me how her husband can run away with other women and that she's quite happy if he's been bumped off. It's not the best cover story I've ever heard and because of that, it might just be truthful. It doesn't mean she didn't kill him though.

'Is there any reason that John Carson would be watching this house?'

She looks at me. 'John Carson?'

'He's watching the house right now. I took a run around before I came in. That's why I came in the back door. He's watching the house.'

She gets up, walks out of the room without switching any further lights on. I hear her go upstairs. It's about three minutes later when she comes back down.

'Is there any reason why he should be watching your house? Has he watched you before?'

'John and I had a few moments, shall we say, in the past, but that's all been over for a while. Russell didn't know about them, either. I'm not my husband, much more discreet. John also has a wife, so that was the other reason for staying quiet. It was just a bit of fun. He knew that. I knew that, so I don't know what he's doing at the moment.'

'Maybe he thinks you're in danger,' I say.

'Me, in danger?'

'Well, yes. Your husband didn't turn up for a game of golf. And he's not here, so what's going on?'

She looks at me, a little worried, and stands up. Exiting the room again, presumably to go and watch out of the window. I'm left with my thoughts. At the moment I have a line of characters and supposed money but not much substance to the characters. They do have all of one thing in common, the golf club, so I feel I may be spending some time up there. I should ask Susan to get me a game with these people, or at least point them out.

Susan's an interesting one at the moment. Very keen on me

and I could use that to my advantage. Just take her golfing for the week, getting her to point out people to me. But sometimes this side of the business can go nasty and that could leave her in a lot of bother. I can always walk away from the situation. This is her life. So as much as the idea of her running around with me for a week appeals, I think I'll keep her at a distance.

After a while, Alison Hadleigh storms back into the room. 'He's still bloody well there. What is he doing? It's like a little perv keeping eyes on me.'

'Why don't you go outside and ask him?' I say.

'What do you mean?'

'Go out and ask him what he's doing,' I say.

'You want me to go on my own?'

'Probably best if you go alone. You know him. I can't dare to be seen, so you go by, see what he's doing and I'll wait here, drinking my wine. Unless you're worried. Of course, if you see that he's going to threaten you or something, I'll be across and sort it. It's not a problem. Can always crack him one.'

She says quickly, 'Don't do that. I think I can handle it.'

She walks off to the front door and I hear her grab a coat. As soon as she's opened the door, I walk quickly out of the room and into a dark dining room, peering from behind the curtains. I see her across the road and John Carson steps out of his car before she even arrives, which is a little unusual if you're trying to watch somebody in secret. She approaches him and he steps forward putting his arms around her, which she pushes back. There's a brief row going on, but it's quiet not blazing. She keeps pointing back towards the house. I didn't get the sound but I can lip read. She's telling him that I'm in there and what is he doing blowing cover like this. Her tale was a lie. He's been there for a reason.

What that reason is, I don't know. They finish off with a quick kiss. She didn't want to step forward for it, but she couldn't back away either. He's obviously no expert in these matters and I watch him drive off as she returns back down the drive quickly. I make my way back into the sitting room, grab my wine, down half of it, and then as she comes in. I sip a little more just to give the impression this is where I've been the whole time.

'Bloody little prick says he's worried about me. Well, I don't believe that for a minute. Maybe he's just not over me.'

'Maybe not,' I say. 'I think I have had enough for tonight—time to get sleep and get up early.'

'You're probably tired. Is your bed comfortable enough?' she asks, 'because if it's not, I've always got other places you could sleep.' It's a pretty blunt come on and I'm trying to work out why she wants to bed a one-armed man. I'm no Adonis. Yeah, I keep in shape, but I don't have the looks, but she seems to keep pushing at me for this. I get up to leave the room. She steps across, but I'm saved by the phone. The ringer chirps several times and I pass the phone to her.

She picks it up as if all is well but I notice there's an anxiousness about her. She's hearing a voice on it that's causing her pain. I hold my hand up to my face indicating whether or not she's got another phone. She points to the far corner where there's an old one. I pick it up and, hold it up to my ear, trying to hold my breath. I'm not like other people who can cover or mute the microphone end. If I did, I'd drop the phone. The voice on the other end is foreign and female. It's fairly high pitched, but it sounds possibly Russian, maybe based somewhere.

A woman says that she has a message from Mr Hadleigh to

his wife. He regrets to say that he's away on business and will be staying out of the country for a while. She's not to worry and he'll be home in a couple of days. I see her go to speak, but the line's been terminated. Alison's shaking and she puts the phone down to turn and look at me.

'He's away on business,' she says 'That's good. He's often on business. He'll come home. Yes.' She says, 'He never told me he was going *on business*—not *on business*. Daft wee bugger.' She says the two words like they mean something.

I touch her shoulder and say, 'I'm going to go up to bed due to an early start in the morning. I'll check out if he really is away *on business*, tomorrow.' But this time she doesn't try and invite me to her bed. She just seems stunned. I leave and start walking up the stairs to my room. I can hear Alison demanding more attention from a telephone buddy.

Chapter 5

I get up at 5 AM. It's an early start as I've got a lot to do today. Taking a quick shower, I'm surprised when I exit the bathroom to find Alison standing there, wrapped in just a towel, about to go in.

'You're up early,' she says.

'Likewise. Are you normally an early riser?'

'No,' she says, 'but I can't sleep. All this issue around Russell, it's not easy to get off. I'm not used to being in a bed alone.'

'Lucky you,' I say, 'I'm well used it,' and walk past her. If I were a more attractive man or had some sort of money or power, I wouldn't be asking myself why she's so keen on me. The thing with Susan is, she's a young girl and maybe she sees a bit of excitement or danger in this man who has just appeared. I'm also a lover of golf so that's what I'm putting her infatuation down to, but Alison has hardly got a reason for trying to take me into that deep confidence. And I don't trust her one bit. I'm not some secret agent who sleeps with the mark and runs around betraying them. Don't think I'd be good at that.

The morning's bright as I leave around six o'clock, having had breakfast. Alison came down and offered to make it for me, swanning about in her dressing gown. Again, I refused, made my own and got out. Now I disappear over the back wall again, running through the neighbours, having to hide momentarily as a man steps out with a briefcase on his way to work. Getting into the car, I drive to a place where I start to do a little bit of research—on my mobile—about the clothing companies around Stranraer. I manage to track down the name Angus Porterfield and his stores seem to have two different brands: one simply called Sarah's seems to cater for an older woman whereas Juno is apparently in the younger market, teens, maybe twenties. That's as far as I can tell not being a fashion guru.

Conducting my research sitting in a coffee shop overlooking Loch Ryan, this part of the world looks glorious in the sun. I fell in love with the sea some time ago and it gives me that calming influence. Back in the day, when I used to be a police officer, I was much more stressed, much more hyped up. It took me years after the bomb blast to come around to this way of living, this way of thinking. When you lose something like an arm, you mourn. You sit there and cry your eyes out for it. It naturally feels like there's a part of you gone but you also learn how to rebuild. And you also have to learn how to let go the anger and the hatred too. Somebody killed a part of me. They just took it. It didn't help that I lost some friends in that blast, too.

I spend a lot of time on the boat looking at the sea and it's always a good friend unless of course, it's trying to throw your boat over sideways because you got out in the stupidest of storms, but normally it gives you that soothing rub to your shoulders. It sits there and listens when you yell at it. Find a woman to do that. Not one has been that much of a friend to me. On the other hand, I haven't exactly looked. It dents your confidence when you lose an arm. I mean what does it look like. What woman would seriously want that, especially with the scars I've got across my back as well? Who would? Well, I never said I healed properly. So, my life is often spent on my own, often spent with the sea beside me.

That's why I came here this morning to work. The place is quiet and the woman who serves me keeps it simple, matter of fact pleasant, but can see that I'm not interested in conversation. She asks what she needs to cook me—a couple of eggs—and lets me get on with it.

I thought I might pop into one of the stores, but I'd like to go and speak to Susan at the club, to see where the best one is. I ring her and she says it's in the middle of Stranraer.

After finding a place to park, I walk up just as it opens at nine o'clock. It is a little bit strange, an older man walking into such a snappy store. But there you go. I don't have time on my side, and I need to examine the shop. It isn't that big, but it certainly knows how to charge. I have an awkward moment of walking into the section for underwear and like any man on his own, I probably seem like some sort of pervert and so desperately head off in a different direction. I pick up some skirts, have a look at the material and then pick up trousers. I look at blazers and some jumpers. The label says they are made in various different countries in Asia, a lot of poorer countries, not China. I purchase a rather smart polo shirt that would be ideal for Susan for golf. I have to guess her size. I'll probably be wrong, and I'll be bringing this back, but there you go. I chat to the woman serving behind the counter, just asking generally where these clothes come from. She says they are all handmade. There's a factory overseas with specially trained seamstresses, but their owner, Mr Porterfield, has made it his place to go out there and set up a foundation. This is somewhere with ethical clothes for ethical people and that's why a lot of the teenagers, the younger people, come in here. Well, look at the prices; he certainly seems to charge the earth. With the polo shirt in hand, I disappear up to the golf club, getting there for about ten o'clock. Walking into the pro shop, I see Susan at the back of it, stocking some boxes. The professional who first greeted me in the shop is there and comes over to ask if he can help.

'I'd like to talk to Susan if that's possible.'

He turns around and tells her to take twenty minutes, smiling broadly. 'She said you're quite handy with a set of clubs. One-armed as well. I'd like to see that sometime.'

'No problem,' I say, 'but I don't play like she plays.'

'Oh, yes, our Susan's doing well. She could really get there if we can get her into the right places.'

Susan smiles, a little embarrassed but tells me to follow her out of the shop. Instead of taking me into the clubhouse, she takes me down a path that leads through a small wooded area where there is a bench. We sit down and I offer her the package I just bought.

'That's great,' she says, 'I'll try it on if you want.' I wasn't quite expecting her to take her top off and throw the next one on and as she starts to lift it, I turn away. I'm from that era when we didn't do things like this. She taps my shoulder and as I turn back, she's laughing.

'You didn't have to do that,' she says.

'I'm brought up to be like that and besides, I didn't know what you were wearing underneath.'

'How does it look?' she says.

'It fits you well. I got it at that Juno's. That's why I was asking earlier.'

'They have some good stuff in there. A lot of my friends like it. It's also got that ethical label with it. It's not one of the Fairtrade ones, it's his own one, one Mr Porterfield does. He's been quite good for the club as well. Quite supportive of me. It's just he's a little bit creepy at times. You know those men that give you that look.'

I shrug my shoulders. 'I don't tend to get looks from a lot of men.'

She laughs. 'Well, trust me; he gives you a look that's creepy. But he's been incredibly supportive in my golf—that's one thing I have to say about him. But we've been here ten minutes already and Iain said I can have twenty. So, what are you looking for?'

'Well,' I say, 'apart from seeing your charming face again, which is always good, I want to know if you can set up some rounds of golf for me.'

She nods, 'Sure, I'll be happy to play with you.'

'Good,' I say, 'but I'd like to play with specific people.'

She looks inquisitive. 'Paddy,' she says, 'can I ask you a question?'

'Sure,' I say, 'fire away.'

'I was hearing today that nobody has seen the judge—nobody has seen Russell Hadleigh anywhere in the last couple of days.'

'Right,' I say, 'that's unusual, is it?'

'It certainly is. I can't remember him being away in the last year like this. I've seen people come and ask me questions and you've shown up. It seems he's in some sort of trouble. Are you some sort of policeman?'

I shake my head. 'I'm not a policeman, Susan, but I am looking for him.' She looks intrigued. 'I was going ask if I can trust you, but I just have.' Again, she smiles, almost blushing. 'Do me a favour. I'm going to ask you to get me a round with some people. Come with me and play those rounds. Make it happen for me. Can you do that?'

Smiling, she reaches out her hand and touches mine. 'You seem like a good guy,' she says. 'Of course, I can. Besides, I want to see that swing again.' She reaches forward and gives me a peck on the cheek.

'Susan,' I say, 'that's where it stays. You're a nice girl, I like talking to you, but we stay at talking. Okay?'

She looks a little disappointed, but she nods okay. Maybe behind that she's hoping I'll mellow. Maybe she thinks I'm working on a case and I haven't got time for her at the moment. Who knows? All those reasons are maybe true. What I do know is I've got to get into some four-balls with people I need to meet. So, I tell her the names, ask her to get me a match with Mr Porterfield, his friend Mr Lasseter, and possibly Laura Sutherland as well.

'Any particular time you want?'

'Sure, if you can make it morning, something that roles into lunchtime, that would be good, as then I have an excuse to invite them back, have lunch and talk more to them. Would you be able to do that—I mean could you get away from the pro shop?'

'They just give me that because they know I won't be up here at the club otherwise. If there's nothing on, I'm out playing rounds all the time. Ian, our pro, is great; he wants to develop me, but he knows I need some sort of a job, so I get a small wage from helping him out. It allows me to play my golf. He also takes me out for lessons at times. But he's saying I'm getting beyond where he's at.'

'You certainly looked like it, one of the best I've played with.' She smiles at this. Her hand comes out again and touches mine. I'm going have to be careful here because she's quite endearing and she seems like a good kid. The last thing I need is for her to get too involved. I walk her back to the pro shop, drop her off, and yet again receive another beaming smile. It's nice to have somebody look at me that way. It's nice to see somebody look at me in any way after Alison Hadleigh's forced effort.

After leaving the Golf Club, I decide I need to look further into this clothing business with Mr Porterfield. Going through the internet, I come up with an address for his offices which seem to be on an estate outside of Stranraer. I drive out to case them and there appears to be a number of compact buildings on the estate. The place isn't busy but there's a couple of cars outside the building with his placard on it. With a pair of binoculars, I read the sign 'Porterfield trading'.

I sit and watch it for an hour or two. Only two people come in and out. There's a tall woman, possibly a secretary, and a man who looked like a financer. Around about lunchtime, they both disappear in cars. I step up to the office. The front door is locked, and it says closed for lunch, back about two o'clock. I look around the estate; it's quiet and I check for cameras. There's one at the front of the building. Walking round to the back, I see another. I've got my prosthetic on again and a change of coats, hopefully looking like a businessman who's just lost.

After walking back a number of times, scanning into windows, I suddenly point to a different building and walk into a fireplace showroom. Inside I make an inquiry about a fictitious house I have, spend twenty minutes in there before coming back out and walking past the cameras again, disappearing off to my car. There's an alarm box as well. I'm going to need help with this one, it's not going to be a case of simply breaking in. I get a change of clothing, pull a large padded envelope out of the boot of the car. I have a number of predesigned outfits, they let me do things on the hoof. And they are perfect for what I am about to do next because I want to get inside that office and see what I'll be breaking into tonight. Having seen the man and the woman return to the office, I make my way over holding a large envelope in my hand. Opening the front door, I arrive at a set of stairs and climb them, entering a room with a large desk and a woman stooped behind it.

'Can I help you?' she asks, standing. 'If you're looking for Mr Porterfield, I'm afraid he's not in town at the moment.'

'Mr Porterfield?' I say. 'No, I'm not looking for Mr Porterfield. I was actually looking to pick up.'

'Pick up?' she says.

'Yes,' I say, 'I've got a pickup from this address, some goods for Liverpool. It said a small package. She looks at me blankly, and no wonder, there's no small package to pick up.

'I'm sorry,' she says, 'I don't understand. We haven't got anything. I don't believe Mr Porterfield's asked for that.'

'Very good,' I say. I've got a baseball cap on and it's tilted, keeping my face away from the camera. I try not to move about too much because my prosthetic looks like a prosthetic if there's too much activity and it stays still.

'Could you ask in the office, just to see if anyone's ordered it, and hasn't let you know?'

She gets quite indignant. 'Well, they wouldn't be doing that; everything that comes out of this office goes through me.'

'Well, I don't mean to be funny, love, but can you ask? It's just if I go away from here and I haven't got it and it was there, then

I inevitably get the blame because somebody doesn't know. So, if you can check for me, it will be much appreciated.'

'Well, there's only the one office in here. Well, that and Mr Porterfield's, but that's locked. Hang on, I'll just go in here and find out for you,' she says. With that, she turns through the door behind her into an office suite. I nonchalantly walk in behind her and in a completely rude fashion, but I get a scan of the office. There are three desks, one of which is occupied by the man; another one looks as if it should be occupied, but no one's there. There's a third one, a number of filing cabinets and beyond this, there's another door, presumably through to Mr Porterfield's office. I can see an open door at the back that leads through to a small kitchen, but otherwise that seems to comprise the entire building.

'Ian, have you ordered a pickup for any parcels?'

'No, Sarah, I haven't. Why? Somebody said there is? I don't think John has either.'

She turns round and suddenly realises I'm standing right behind her. 'You have to go back to reception,' she says. 'You're not meant to be in here.'

'Sorry love, I just followed you through to see. But thanks for checking though, much appreciated.' And off I go. I can feel her annoyance as I make my way down the stairs. Maybe there's a bit of a storeroom underneath, maybe that's why the offices are up above but there are certainly cameras inside the offices. Maybe there will be a camera inside his room. I'm going to need to get my contacts here, and quick.

Walking back to my car, I go through my head who I need and then I drive off, finding a bench somewhere near the sea with a good signal on the mobile. I pick up one of my extra SIM cards—the ones I use only once. Pressing it inside, I dial a number. The voice that comes back speaks with a German accent. 'Hans, it's your favourite one-armed employer,' I say. 'Where are you?' He's in London. 'Get a flight, Hans, a flight to Glasgow. I'll pick you up at eight o'clock.'

Chapter 6

I really should be getting some sleep. When you perform a break-in in the middle of the night and don't sleep the night before, you're going to suffer. I don't really want to go back to Alison's because if I do and she's there how do I explain going to sleep in the middle of the afternoon. I also don't trust her having seen her rather dubious conversation with John Carson who she claims to be having problems with. I actually wonder why she hired me and what she's at. Until she tells me more, she's being kept on the end of an exceptionally long stick. Her overtly forward intentions, parading with not very much on in front of me has also made me suspicious. It's very crass, certainly not subtle, and has my back up.

So, I take the car to a country park, finding a car park within it, away from the others. I drive under the shade of a large tree and get into the back of the car when my mobile goes off. Part of me wants to leave it but then I notice it's Susan's number and she may have some information.

'Hello there,' I say; 'what's happening?'

'Got some news for you, Paddy. Looks like Laura Sutherland is up for a four-ball tomorrow. Seems like half the group cancelled, so I stuck my nose in and asked if she needed some company. She has agreed. She was trying to get me to play with one of the other members, but I said I had a friend in town. So, you and I are up for a four-ball tomorrow, eight a.m. sharp. You okay with that?'

I'm not okay with that at all. It will be hard going after being up most of the night, but I can't reject an opportunity like this. 'That's brilliant! Do you know who her partner is?'

'Not personally,' she says, 'it's a foreign guy. I think his name is Sergei. Lasseter is his surname. Haven't really seen him myself but I think the judge played with him once. Anyway, you'll see him tomorrow. What are you doing right now?' she says.

'Not a lot,' I reply. 'I'm just trying to rest up to be honest.'

'Why, you got some hot date tonight?' she teases.

'No, just got a bit of business on.'

'Are you up for a meet? Would you take a girl for an ice-cream sundae?'

I should really say no. I need to sleep. I've got this on, but part of me thinks this might be the only fun I get in the next couple of days. And it has been a while since I had a bit of fun. And I mean innocent fun, just to chat. She golfs like me, so we have plenty to talk about. And I might be able to stay strictly off the case for a couple of hours because to be honest; my head starts to swim if I get involved too much in it. 'Okay then,' I say, 'but I can't stay for long. Where do we go?'

'Pick me up on the way into Stranraer,' she says, 'and then you can take me out to the country parks. Looks like it's going to be nice this afternoon.' She tells me a street corner, and I heartily agree, getting back into the front of my car and driving back into Stranraer. I circle around a little bit, so I am coming towards her as if I've been in town the whole time.

I see her smiling face as I drive along, and pull over, reaching across to throw open the door. She's wearing a light summer top, short skirt, and some trainers as she steps in. Her red hair is tied up behind her and she's all smiles. We talk about next to nothing as we drive out of Stranraer. She points me towards a little forest trail that I'm unaware of. Because of the time of year, the trees look lush as we walk along in the cool of the shade. It's mostly banal comments about last year's Open or the American circuit and I realise just how knowledgeable she is about her own sport.

When we walk, I keep her on my left-hand side. That way my arms look right. She can't grab my hand. A couple of times she puts her hand on my shoulder, which is fine. But I'm determined to keep that distance. As we walk, we come out of the forest into the edge of a large field. There is a small bench there and she indicates that we should sit down. I reach it first, plonk myself in the middle of the bench and wait for her. But she moves behind it and flings her arms around my shoulders, her chin resting on the back of my head.

'You're quite different, aren't you, Paddy,' she says. Something in me wonders if she's a bit more than she says. 'Kirsten says so, too—a right charmer when you were talking to her.'

'Well, a man tries his best.'

'I think my mother would freak if she knew I was out here with you like this.'

'Like what? We're just a couple of friends out having a walk. You know that, don't you?'

'Yes,' she says. 'I know you keep putting me off and I keep trying to tell myself that you're not simply trying to use me to get into the golf club.'

While it's true there is that element, there is a side to this that is about my own personal enjoyment. It's nice to have someone to talk to. You see, life on my boat and investigating is usually pretty lonely. So, for once I try to be honest.

'Susan, I'm not just trying to get into the golf club and I'm also maybe trying not to think too much. You're great fun and great company. You should think of me as a big brother, not merely what you want to think of me. If you can't manage that, maybe we shouldn't be disappearing off into the forest like this.'

She laughs. 'That's the problem, Paddy; if you turned round and said it was a lot more, I would be so wary and put off. A man just trying to see what he can get. But when you start saying you want to be a friend and act like it, it makes me want the other type of person even more.' She drops a kiss on the back of my head, and I have to admit for a moment I'm really quite taken. But there's another place I need to be, and definitely another she needs to be.

'Are you okay with that, just friends? Nothing more than friends, but good friends.' I stand up and turn around to catch her look which is one of disappointment. She smiles though and says, 'Yes.' I think she means it.

We walk back to the car because I really do need to go and get some sleep. But when we reach it, she insists on taking me off to an ice-cream shop and we sit for another hour gassing away about the final rounds in the majors and even having an in-depth conversation all about the women's game before I realise I need to get to Glasgow and pick up Hans. So, I make my excuses and take Susan back into town before my planned trip to Glasgow. As she closes the door, she turns around and knocks the window. I move it down using the button and she leans in. 'If there's a reason you're in the golf club, more than just having fun right now,' she says, 'you know you can tell me.

You can trust me!'

I look at her. I wonder if she knows what she's asking. 'Why do you say that?'

'First, you're talking about the judge; then you're talking about Laura Sutherland, and Angus Porterfield as well. You're asking a lot of questions about people at times, Paddy. And you want to get close and meet them. Some of these characters are not that savoury and there are rumours around the club about them, and to be honest, it makes me a little fearful and wonder what you are. If you want to tell me you can; in fact, I think you may owe me it given what I'm doing for you.'

'And if I was a person looking into these people,' I say, 'not that I am saying I am, if I did tell you, whatever it was I was doing, would that not put you more at risk?' She looks at me, her smile gone and a serous grimace on her face. 'That wouldn't be much of a big brother effort, would it? That wouldn't be much of a friend who put you at risk?'

Her smile comes back. 'But you can trust me,' she says. 'I hope you know that. Someday tell me who you really are and what you're about. Because I want to know Paddy, not this persona you are going with at the moment.'

For her years she's got a lot of intuition and I have to fight to stop myself telling her to get back in, take her somewhere, and tell her everything to see where it runs. But my own statement holds. If I don't know what I'm walking into myself, I certainly shouldn't take someone by the hand and lead her in with me. So, I give her a smile and say, 'One day.' This seems to appease her, and she blows a kiss through the window saying eight o'clock in the morning and that my game better be up to it.

I am late as I pick up Hans. This is not unusual. He's well used to waiting for me and shows little annoyance as I wave to him from my car. He climbs in and we drive back to Ayr, en route to Stranraer from Glasgow airport, where we stop off for a quick bite to eat.

It's about nine o'clock now and I start detailing out the plans for the break in, telling him I'll drop him in position by the offices and leave him for a few hours to secure the alarm systems. I can usually manage simple break-ins myself, simple house alarms, basic locks to pick but the offices are a bit more special than that and Hans will keep me safe. He comes with a charge, but he does know what he's doing.

How do I know Hans? Let's just say I arrested him once, a long time ago. He was quite young heading down a path that would either lead to glory, or end with a long time in jail. I managed to nip him in the bud before he headed off down the jail path, and ever since, he's been grateful. Grateful enough to come out to do these jobs on the wrong side of the law for me.

It's about half past eleven when I drop him off and the night's a cool one. That's the thing about clear skies in the summer. Some of the nights can actually be quite nippy in this part of the world. I leave him alone for a couple of hours, telling him I will return about two o'clock to make my entry. He nods and I disappear to park up, taking myself into the back seat, trying to go to sleep. It's not a task that's that easy. I wind up thinking about the case, thinking about Alison, and what she's up to. I'm wondering why the judge hasn't been reported in as missing. But there is another part that keeps coming back and focusing on Susan. That's probably not healthy. I told her she needed to be in that friend's spot and that's where I need to make sure I see her as well.

Returning to Hans, I find him in a bush across the industrial estate. No one has been near the office, in fact, no one's been near the industrial estate, a quiet little outpost of Stranraer. He says he has the alarms on tap, and I am good to go as soon as I give the nod. Handing me a tiny microphone and earpiece setup, we test communications. I'm no good with all this stuff and having someone who knows what to do has helped me many times in the past.

I don a mask, dress in black, and head for the front door. He tells me the cameras are disabled and the door's open for me. It's true and I walk up the stairs round to that first office. Again, he says the cameras are disabled. What he's actually doing is replaying the image that's been recorded for the last hour, so their tapes are picking it up.

I walk through the office and head for the smaller office at the back that should belong to Angus Porterfield. The door's locked, but this is a simple lock. There are no wires attached to the door system. I break out my lockpick tools and it takes me maybe five minutes to open the door. In fairness, Hans could probably be though this door in about thirty seconds but that's the difference. He's an expert, albeit with two hands, I'm an amateur—that's why he's here.

The office has one large desk with a leather chair behind it. On one wall are pictures of children while another has photographs of a man holding black kids, others of him holding Asian kids. Some of these photographs show pieces of machinery, fabric being worked on. I go to a large filing cabinet, again locked at the top, and it takes me five minutes to break into that. I look at files which are basic accounting files. Struggling to make head or tail of them, I take out a small camera and start photographing. I need to sit down at some point and look through them. Or maybe I'll get my experts onto it. There's more cabinets and I work my way through, capturing each item in turn. My hands are gloved so I leave no fingerprints. With the hood on my head and the black clothing, I shouldn't leave any hairs either.

Not that they should have cause to search or think about that, as I have put everything back in its place. After spending an hour taking a multitude of photographs of the printed paper, I attach a dongle onto the side of the computer and switch it on. This is linked out to Hans and hopefully he should be able to break in and take some details as well. Meantime I set to work on the office desk picking at the lock on the side and start to open the drawers.

In the top one is a series of photographs. I recognise John Carson in one of them and also Alison Hadleigh. They are clinched together, and it looks quite passionate. There is also a photograph of Laura Sutherland. I know this because it's annotated. Brunette, long layered hair, quite the figure and she's standing holding a golf club with a man who has a Russian appearance beside her. I don't recognise him. At least I haven't seen him up at the club, but he looks like a thug. I work down the drawers and find a pile of money in the middle one. I don't take it out and count it individually but there looks like there must be nearly twenty grand there. It's a funny place to keep it.

The bottom drawer has more envelopes, some writing with some letterheads, and I photograph that. At the bottom of the pile is a packet of photographs, again, John Carson and Alison Hadleigh. You might remember that Alison was waiting in just a dressing gown for me, trying to catch my eye. Well these photographs are far worse. They look like they have been photographed without the subject's knowledge as well, and the two of them are in the full throes of entertaining each other shall we say.

I stop, sitting my haunches for a minute, thinking. Why am I here? Why am I pulled in to investigate this? Is she being blackmailed? And where is the judge and what has he got to do with it? I get a message in my ear that Hans has all the details he can find on the computer. I pull out the dongle as he switched it off remotely. He'll have cleaned up, not that I know how he does that. I tidy up my affairs, lock everything up again and get back out of the office.

It's now about four-thirty and I need to drop Hans back to the airport and then get back to town, then I'm back on the golf course at eight. Once I finish my round, I'll need to get into looking at these papers, but I should be able to send them off to some associates I have, to see if there's anything of interest.

The dawn is coming up as I drop off Hans, who shakes my hand and says he'll send the files through from the computer direct to my other associates. I nod, thank him, turn around, and drive the car back through Ayr and onto Stranraer. I change in a layby into my golf gear and it is ten minutes to eight when I drive up and park the car. I take the clubs out of the boot; in all honesty, shattered, as I walk up, golf bag over my shoulder, and see some red hair and a bright smile that cheers me up no end.

'You ready for some golf, Paddy?'

I smile. 'Am I ever ready for golf!'

Chapter 7

I've got that feeling in my bones. The one where you just haven't had any sleep and it feels like your legs are sore, aching, and you're struggling to move. Despite Susan, I still feel lethargic. I'm hoping I can bring my game today. I know I'm investigating but when you've got that competitiveness in you, it never goes away. I stop into the Pro Shop, pick up some drinks, and I get myself a few chocolate bars, something to keep me going, because I haven't had any breakfast yet. Susan laughs as she watches me wolf them down.

'Have you got worms or something?' she says. 'I'm sure you've only just got up and had something to eat. Looks like you've had a fun night.' At first she smiles at this, then it looks like something dawns on her in the back of her head. Then she frowns. She goes to ask me another question, but then stops.

'What's the matter?' I ask.

'I was just wondering what was keeping you up all night.'

I say, 'Didn't really sleep that well.' She smiles, seemingly happy with this answer. Then her face becomes sullener as into the Pro Shop walks a brunette woman. She's dressed in smart green trousers with pink and gold shoes. On top, she has a rather smart body warmer leaving her arms only covered by the short sleeves of the polo shirt. The woman is beaming broadly and looking over at Susan.

'Well, good morning to you,' she says. 'Is this the gentleman we're playing with?' And then she turns to me extending her hand. I reach out with mine and shake it. 'Sorry to be so forward, but given your . . . How shall we say, single-armedness, I could tell it was you. Is it Paddy?' I shake the hand vigorously.

'Yes, it's Paddy, and you must be Laura,' I say. 'Delighted to meet you.' I've got my best voice on, and the woman has a way of engaging you. She picks up a few things from the shop, and together we head out towards the first tee where Laura says her companion will be joining us. Sure enough, there's already a man there. He has an Eastern European look about him and he's well built. In another life, if he had a black jacket on standing outside a club, he could be a bouncer anywhere, but here he looks like a sportsman overbuilt for his game. He's too muscular for a golfer. I guess we'll see how he gets on.

'Paddy, Susan, this is Sergei, a business friend visiting so it's quite appropriate that we've met you on this day to show Sergei some of the best sport we have. He does play a bit socially, but I'm afraid you'll be giving us a few shots. I take it we're happy to play four-balls match play? How's your game Paddy? I know Susan's is stunning.'

I explain I'm off ten.

'Let me calculate how many shots we're giving them a hole,' says Susan

It turns out it's at least one, and often two, which playing four-ball can make it a tough match, but I've got to remember my other side today, I'm here to investigate Laura's relationship with the judge. On the first tee, Sergei hooks his first shot into the trees on the left-hand side. Susan as ever cracks hers straight down the middle. Mine heads off to the light rough on the right, which coincidentally is where Laura's ball ended up, too. It's almost as if I placed it there. With Susan heading off to help Sergei look for his ball, I get to walk alongside Laura.

'I can't help but think your name's familiar,' I say. 'I don't know where I'm hearing it from. Maybe there's people at the club here I know that you know.'

She smiles. 'Well, that's always a possibility. Who are you thinking of?'

'Well, I'm up here trying to do a little bit of work, but I got recommended the course by a judge called Russell Hadleigh who I met at a conference.' I can see the flicker in her eyes, but she's very calm, very controlled. 'Do you know Russell?'

'I do know Russell,' she says. 'We have quite a long history.'

'Oh?' I say. 'How's that then?'

'Russell was my golf partner here for quite a while. We played a large number of rounds together, even got well placed in a couple of the club tournaments. But I haven't seen him lately, it's almost like he's disappeared. He's a very dear man. Very polite, but extremely competitive. A bit like myself.'

I decide to venture a compliment to see if I can draw her out. 'Well, it's quite obvious why he would want to play with you.'

'Is it?'

'Well, yes,' I say. 'Even after the first shot I can see what a decent swing you've got. I'm sure the conversation's great as well.'

She smiles, but she's pretending to be flattered. Underneath it I can tell she's wondering who I am. 'Tell me a little bit more about yourself. What line of work is it that you're in, Mr Smythe?'

'Paddy. Always Paddy. I work around investigative techniques, new types of scanners, quite often working with powders as well. It's all to do with the techniques that are used by forensics. I freelance doing supply for them, so hence I have a connection into a lot of the worlds of law enforcement.'

Whilst the story isn't true, it always gives me a good connection in case I spot anyone I know from the right side of the law. When you're undercover and suddenly a policeman walks up and says, 'Hi Paddy,' it never goes down well, and as low a profile as I try to keep in my day-to-day business, you always meet people from the past and it's not fair just to send them out of the way. A cover like this always means you can explain away why you know so many police officers.

'Forensics? That must be a fascinating field,' she says, the smile staying, and she walks off to hit her next shot. It's after I've hit mine that I decide to throw in the bombshell and right here on the first hole because it should give me plenty of time to have a discussion further round. I've shouldered my bag, stepped across to walk beside Laura, up the right-hand side of the fairway. Susan seems to be assisting Sergei whose ball doesn't seem to want to find the green at all.

'I think I know you now,' I say to Laura. 'One of the conferences, it was late at night. We'd had a few beers and that, and I got to talking to the judge about people he knew. I mean, people he really liked. That's where your name came up. So, the description was right. We kept on going on about your legs as well. Sorry, that's a bit forward. I'm just thinking about where I knew him from, but I can certainly see why he brought you up. Although, forgive me, it wasn't the golf he was talking about.'

There was a bit of a blush, but it was possibly put on. She smiled and looked at me. 'Well, we did have our moments.

Although, please, don't let that get out anywhere else. You do know he's married?'

'Oh yes, he said so to me, but I'm not sure it sounded that great a marriage. He seemed to talk more about you.'

'Oh, and what did he say?'

'Well, to be honest, I can't repeat most of it, but it did sound quite serious. Were you really serious at any point?'

The woman shakes her head, her layered brunette hair moving in unison, possibly due to the lacquer applied to it. 'No, Paddy, I'm very much available. I haven't had a serious relationship in the last twenty years. That's maybe from a broken heart, but I like my man to be there available for me. Doesn't pay to get too close to people. What about yourself? I take it you're not playing around with the young girl over there, attractive as she is—a little bit too young for yourself.'

And so, the conversation continues, a lot of jibes and awfully familiar tones. It isn't until we are on the twelfth hole that I am able to corner Sergei. We are stood at the back of the green, having found his ball yet again, which seems to refuse to land anywhere near where the pin is. We are waiting for Laura and Susan who are stranded in the same bunker.

'Are you enjoying the Royal Cairns, Sergei?' I ask.

'It's amazing to see somebody play with one arm. The way you hold the club, how do you do that?' he asks.

'It's like everything in life, you get used to it.'

'And you've been like that since birth?

I shake my head. "I lost it in an explosion," I say, failing to mention that I was part of the security forces when it happened. "One of the hazards of living in a country that's on the edge."

"I understand it," he says. His English is broken, very understandable, but broken. "In my country too we had to play around the law, but it makes you strong. It makes you understand business. Makes you understand how to take things."

'I would say the opposite, Sergei. I'm very live and let live.'

He slaps me on the back. 'Maybe, but you,' he says, 'you're a man who understands what he wants.' With that he nods over towards Susan.

I shake my head. 'No, she's just helping my golf. Too young for me.'

'Well, speak for yourself.'

It's a tone I don't like, and I try to take the conversation away from it, even though my professional side thinks I might explore it. There's a hut at the back of the twelfth, and I'm not sure what it's for. It's old, looks run down, and there's padlocks on it. I mention this for only one reason, Sergei keeps looking at it. His head flicks round, and it's almost as if he's checking it.

As I'm walking up to the next hole, this time with Susan beside me, I ask her about it.

'Oh, that,' she says. 'That's an old hut. I think there's old flags and stuff stored in it. Nothing of note, anyway. There was talk about getting rid of it, but there was a block put on it. Angus Porterfield said something about not having the funds, and underneath there was concrete that would have to be dug out. It was better to just leave it as it was. They suggested doing it up, but he said it wasn't to be touched. It all seemed a bit strange because I don't think the club's strapped for finances. Well, we're in as good a position as any club.' I make a note of the comment. I'm thinking if I've got spare time, I should come back and have a look at that hut.

My golf today is not great, although Sergei seems impressed

that I can even hit the ball with my one arm. Fortunately, Susan's on form, and I tell her so as she drains many putts to keep us in the game. Laura is particularly useful with the extra shots she's getting from Sergei's rather poor game. The match stays close down to the last. My arms are aching as we tee off down the long par five, and it's the distinct edge to the game that's surprising. Sergei seems to be very up for it, encouraging Laura on despite the fact that his own golf sees him lose two balls a hole.

Susan seems to be getting quite nervous too, and her second shot is slightly off to the right. We're giving away a shot, and when I see Laura's second racing down the middle of the fairway leaving her a chip to the green, I'm under a little bit of pressure to get my second onto said green. Luckily, it's one of my best shots of the day, ending up with a twenty-foot putt. As we continue to walk along looking for Susan's ball, I see her get anxious.

'It's going to be down to you, Paddy. I think you're going to need to drop that.' Sure enough, we have difficulty finding Susan's ball, and when we've run into our time limit, which is strictly enforced by Laura, Susan heads back, hits an extra ball down the fairway, and we end up on the green with Laura there in three, just outside my ball. She putts, comes up short, but close enough to give her the par, leaving me with a putt to win the match. But it's a long one, and as I bend down looking behind it, Susan comes up behind me, hand on shoulder, talking to me about how it's going to swing this way and that.

'Susan, just let me be. I know you can read it, so can I, so let's just let it be.' I think about throwing the putt, ending in a sporting draw, but I reckon Sergei will take us back down to first again to try and get a result, and my legs are sore, my arms are aching, and I really need something to eat. So, I focus hard. It's actually probably the best putt I hit all day, and when I see it drop into the hole, Susan runs towards me. She jumps, throwing her arms around me, giving a little squeal of delight. It's a little bit over the top, and she whispers in my ear, 'Well done, Paddy,' as I to try to hold onto her with one arm.

We shake hands and it's all very friendly. I ask if we can have a bite of lunch. Laura and Sergei agree. As we head up to the club house, Susan goes inside to make arrangements for us. We end up on a balcony outside due to the bright sunshine of the day, and after devouring a rather large golfer's fry, Sergei and Laura excuse themselves, saying they have business to take care of and that they enjoyed the game, but have to hurry along. Susan asks what I'm doing that day, which puts me in a little bit of an awkward spot, but I tell her I need to head off quickly because I have business, too. Sergei and Laura have a start.

When I see the vehicles pull out of the car park, I clock a number plate for Laura. As I jump in my own car, I drive off quickly trying to catch up with at least one of the two cars that have disappeared. It's only as I'm driving out back towards Stranraer that I realize someone's tailing me. It's a black mini, and it's trying to stay at a distance behind me but doing it very badly. I can see the car every time I look in my mirror, and as soon as I overtake anyone on the road, it follows me as well.

This is getting awkward because I watch Sergei pull away and turn off down into a country lane. I follow behind, just about seeing him turn around corners before he disappears into a farm. I drive on past, the mini still behind me. I'm not familiar with the countryside so I don't want to get too far away from the farm where I've seen Sergei's car pull into. As I turn in to a car park for a local walk, I park up as the black mini pulls in alongside. It stops, having parked away from me and facing the opposite direction. I get out of my car, shut the door, and simply walk over to it, rapping the driver's window. When the window rolls down, I see a smiling face with red hair. 'Following me?' I say, 'You're actually following me?'

'You said you had business, and I wanted to know where you were going. Everybody seemed to head off together.'

'But you followed me. I think we've had words before Susan, about you and me and where we're at.' It's then I hear another car coming. I know Susan has been following me but I wonder if anybody's been following her. Stepping into her car, I sit on top of her in the driver's seat and shut her door. The windows on the mini are tinted, which is fortunate, so no one can see inside.

'Hey, what are you doing?' she says.

'Shush,' and I try to struggle over to the passenger seat. Sure enough, a rather stocky man is now in the car park looking around, and he walks over towards Susan's car. 'Quick,' I say, 'Embrace me, wrap me.' I reach over with my one arm, pulling her close. Between half closed eyes, I see someone looking in the tinted windows, and pretend not to notice him. Susan moves her arms around my shoulders, and I pretend to be nibbling her ear. The man seems satisfied and walks off.

'What's all that about?' she says. 'I'm not complaining, Paddy, but what was all that about?'

'I'm going to find out. Stay here.'

'No way,' she says. 'I'm not staying here on my own.'

'Well, drive then. Drive the car away.' I realize this might not be the best option for me because if anybody's still watching, they're going to wonder why I'm still walking off in a different direction having just given the impression that Susan and myself are there for some sort of romantic liaison.

'I'm not leaving you. Something's weird going on here.' And I see her start to shake a little. We should just leave because I shouldn't involve her, should just let this lead go, but who knows how long Sergei is going to be here, and I want to know what they're doing out in this farmyard. So, I turn to her, 'Look Susan, you can come with me, but you keep your mouth shut and you do exactly as I say. And I warn you, you might see something you don't want to.'

'Like what?' She says.

'I don't know. That's why I need to go and find out.'

But she reaches over and takes my hand. 'I'll be quiet,' she says. 'Just don't disappear on me.'

I nod my head. Too right I won't disappear. This little bit of undercover work just got a little bit more awkward.

Chapter 8

Approaching the farmhouse would normally be easy, but when you've got a passenger in tow, it makes it more difficult. Neither of us are particularly dressed for infiltration work, Susan in her culottes, bare shins showing and her polo shirt, and me in my trousers and best golfing gear. I skirt around through fields, keeping close to hedges and keeping hold of Susan's hand with my own. She's trembling inside, but she's also a little excited, possibly a little giddy. It must be quite exciting from her point of view. I know she likes me, and then suddenly I've got this other side to my life, dangerous, and she probably doesn't understand how dangerous it can be. That's a good thing.

It's a decent-sized farm, but there seems to be a lack of people around it today. There's no moving machinery, but I spot at least three or four goons dressed in black and looking similar to the bouncer who came and checked us out in the car. Hopefully, if anybody goes back, they'll think we've run off, getting up to no good in the woods. There could be awkward conversations later with other people, but I'll take that, while we're up to no good trying to find out what's going on. As I cut back through the hedgerow and kneel down behind it, I bring Susan in close. She's kneeling in front of me and I've got an arm on her shoulder, whispering in her ear.

'Listen very carefully. I don't want to leave you here because those guys out there, if they find you, will not be pleasant. However, I need to go inside and find out what's going on. The two people we were playing golf with today are having a meeting our here, guarded like this, so you can guess they're up to no good. I have a feeling Sergei is not just some normal businessman. So, I need you to stay quiet, Susan, and I need you to trust me all the way, doing exactly what I say, when I say it. Do you understand me?'

She turns around, looking at me with big, green eyes. 'Okay, Paddy,' she says. 'And I do trust you.' She leans forward and gives me a peck on the cheek. I really don't need this sort of affection at this time, I just need compliance. But it's hard not to feel something for her. That being said, she's my charge; she's out here and she shouldn't be.

While the farm isn't that big, it's not easy to guard it with the number of people he seems to have with him. I can see Sergei's vehicle parked up, and beside it is Laura's. Outside of that, I only see one other vehicle. Given that Sergei came alone, there's five of them at most. Five guards. One was out looking for us, and will surely be running the perimeter, and the other four will be inside the farm. I spot one walking around the building. Maybe two outside, maybe two inside. I take Susan's hand, move further along until we're in the clear and the guard has disappeared around the corner, and then run towards a large barn. Stepping inside, it's dark, full of straw. I make a way across to the other side, dragging Susan with me. Fortunately, she's got trainers on, nothing stupid like heels. But then a door opens at one end of the barn and I pull Susan down into the straw with me. I hear a grunt and the door closes again, but she's trembling, shaking like anything.

'I'll keep you safe. You're doing well so far.' I say, trying to be encouraging. I get up on my feet, offering her my hand, and take her to the door. Pulling it back, I make sure the coast is clear and then run to the edge of the main farmhouse, rather than approach the front door. I skirt around to the side, carefully looking inside and, seeing no one, I open it. I step inside with her and gently shut it.

There are voices upstairs, but I also hear movement downstairs. I grab Susan and pull her out of the line of sight of the door across from the kitchen we have entered. The footsteps are coming this way, and I pull Susan down, hiding behind a central table. I try to curl up under it, pulling Susan in close and clasping my hand across her mouth as she starts to shake.

'Just stay calm, girl. Just stay calm.' I see a pair of black trousers and feet walk around the kitchen and then back out again. They don't stop because they're on patrol. And who seriously would look under the table? We get back out and, as I look around the open door, I see the man disappear, then grab Susan, running over to the stairs. I give a quick glance up them and slowly, I climb them. I can hear voices up top, those of Sergei and Laura. As I pop my head around onto the landing, I see a goon at the door of a room, but he's looking the other way. There's another bedroom across from us and, grabbing Susan, we quickly sneak across and into it. Once inside, we see a double bed and a wardrobe closest to the wall of the room Sergei and Laura are in. Quickly I take Susan over, open the door, and we step inside the wardrobe. It's pitch black inside, and I can still feel her shaking, so I wrap my arm around her waist, pulling her close and whisper in her ear, 'Just stay calm and quiet, because I'm ready to listen.'

The voices next door are not quiet, but instead raised in anger. 'This is a neat line of work for my bosses,' says Sergei. 'They don't like complications. What were you thinking?'

'It wasn't me,' said Laura. 'I'm just cleaning the mess up.'

'And a mess it is. Do you know what happens if people investigate this? They will close it, they will close the entire line and they will close you and everyone involved. I do not want to see you hurt. You are too pretty a lady to be hurt, but if they ask, then I will close you all down.'

'But you're not stopping the shipments. If you stop the shipments, then there'll be no point. We will close down, we will leave. We cannot make the money without it, and you need an outlet.'

'They have multiple streams. Closing down one to start another will not bother them,' he says. 'But, yes, the shipments continue for now. We will bring them here. We will bring them here as normal and you will continue as normal. That is agreed. But you will also sort out the problem by tonight.'

'And what do you want me to do with it?' Says Laura. 'I'm not akin or used to disposal. Maybe you are, but I don't dispose of people in routine fashion.'

'Now listen here, I am not here to sort out all of your problems. You have been told what to do. Take it, burn it, make sure nothing is left. If you have bones, throw them in the water, water where no one will look. Bury them, bury them under house, under patio, I care not. But tonight, do not leave him where he is. I look today and it is not safe. You have old padlock on door. It is no good.'

'Okay,' said Laura. 'I will do. I will sort it out for you, but that shipment needs to come in. Send it now, and in two days' time we will pick it up here to do the repackaging.'

'And you have everything ready for that?'

'Yes.'

'And the people are ready?'

'You don't understand, this is summer—this is when we make most of the money. In our shops, they do not stop. It goes out the door. Clothing upon clothing.'

The conversation ends abruptly, and everyone seems to leave the building. I stay in the wardrobe with Susan, who's still shaking. After twenty minutes, when I'm happy that everyone's gone, I step out of the wardrobe. It's only then I realize just how much she's been sweating. She's shaking and nervous.

'What were they talking about, Paddy?'

'They're talking about something you should know less about,' I say. 'Forget what you've heard. Do not to talk to anyone about it.' But she looks up to me with scared eyes.

'Get me out of here. Take me back.'

'In a moment, I will. First, we're going to have a quick look around this farmhouse and the surrounding buildings.' I take her to a window and look down to where the cars were parked, but they're gone. Even the car for the goons has gone, but that doesn't mean that they haven't left someone. I sneak downstairs, listening intently, and search the entire house, but find no one. I hold my hands to my lips in case there's any listening devices, but I doubt it. The last thing they want is to record themselves, especially talking about something like this. The farmhouse sits in the middle of several other buildings. One, we were in and was basically bales of straw, but there's two smaller buildings on the far side that I want to examine. It's now late afternoon, and, as I make my way across, pulling Susan with me, we come to a door with a large padlock on it.

'I guess we can't get in here, then,' says Susan. But I shake my head, again holding up my finger to my lips, indicating she should stay quiet. Reaching inside my pockets, I get my basic lock pick, as this is not a difficult lock. Two minutes later, we're inside the building.

I'm amazed at what I see. Piled up in one corner are large cardboard boxes. There're plastic bags within these boxes. They have the word 'Juno' written on them. Now, they shouldn't be here. Why would you have a lot of boxes like this? There's also a number of tables, and it looks like a room where things are simply packaged. But there's at least ten to twelve desks. That's up to twenty-four people who could be coming here to work. There's tape and fake labels. Check sheets that indicate things have been processed correctly, quality assured, but the writing on them, some of them, it's not English. Instead it's a foreign language, indicating other places. But there is no clothing, there is nothing to be packed here at the moment.

We check through to the next building and find it to be empty. There are large wooden doors at the far end, and inside there's a forklift truck. This looks like an operation room for bringing things in, but who is Sergei working for? And where are things coming from? Juno labels up as fairly traded, everything by the book. It's what the teens like. But something is wrong here.

Susan keeps shaking on my arm, telling me we should go. And now I think she's right. Making sure everything is closed up again, we sneak out and head back to our hedgerow. As we come up towards the carpark, I see the black car of the goons. It too has tinted windows and I know what it's doing. It's wondering where we are. I tell Susan we need to head for the path that led out into the forest and act as if we've come from there. I dishevel my clothes, hers too. I explain that these guys will think we have been out into the woods for a liaison, a physical one, and therefore we need to look out of breath. I tell her we're going to walk into the carpark, we're going to embrace strongly, yes, and then get into our separate cars and drive off. I tell her where to drive to and where I'll find her. It's a small café on the outskirts of Stranraer. I tell her to go in there, order something to eat, and I will come and find her and check that she's clear before we meet up again. She's shaking as I tell her this, but I think she's listening.

Five minutes later we're strolling into the carpark and we walk over to her car. She's opening the door when I spin her around, embracing her roughly and kissing her before she gets into the car and drives off. I don't even look at the other black car that's sitting there. Instead, I walk off with a large smile on my face, getting into my own car and driving. The black car follows me, tailing me along, which is good, because it means they're not tailing Susan. I drive to the sports centre I was in when first accosted by Alison to get involved in this. I go inside and take a swim for half an hour. When I come back out, the black vehicle is gone. I'll need to keep an eye on it because they may not be satisfied with how I've run from this. I drive into Stranraer, park up, and then walk to the outskirts, making for the café where I see a half-eaten plate of food sitting in front of Susan. She smiles as I come in, but it's a fearful smile. I sit down beside her, looking around and making sure no one else is in the café I recognize. There are certainly no Russian-type goons.

'Are you okay?' She nods. 'Anybody follow you?' She shakes her head. 'Good. They followed me, but I suspected they would. I need to go.'

'Where?' she says.

'You don't need to know,' I say. 'It's better you're kept out of this now.'

'But what were they talking about, Paddy? It sounded like . . .'

I hold up my hand. 'Not here. And don't think about it. Go home, and don't think about it.'

'They were talking about the hut at the golf club, weren't they?'

'Why do you say that?' I ask.

'Because he was looking at it today and so was Laura. She mentioned it to me when I was on the course, talking about how it just looked like the way it always did. But I hadn't been speaking about it.'

'How long's that hut been there?'

'Years,' she said, and I see her hand shaking on the table. 'But there seemed to be a lock on it I didn't recognize. You don't think?'

'In my line of work, you don't think—you find out. And I'm going to find out now.'

'Don't leave me,' she said. 'Not now.'

'I don't think you want to go where I'm going.' But as I get up, she follows me. I was going to walk back into town, but instead I get into her car and she drives me towards the golf club. 'There's an easier way out to the twelfth,' she says as we're passing down a country lane. She pulls in beside a waste treatment facility, and I get out and follow her down a path, which, sure enough, brings us out into the parkland of the course, right at the back of the twelfth green.

The light's starting to fade now, and there's no one on the course. I walk up to the hut and find the new padlock she's talking about, breaking into it in a matter of minutes. Again, it's not a useful one. But as I open the door, I'm starting to get the bad smell.

'You don't want to look in here, Susan,' I say. As I step into the dark, I use the light from my mobile phone to look around. In front of me are a number of old gardening implements, just looking like an old green keeper's hut. I move some of them back, and there's a plastic bag beneath me. Beside it, there are a number of other plastic bags and I wonder if Laura's even aware of how the person was put here. I know what I'm expecting. As I pick up one plastic bag, I realize it weighs about the weight of a head.

'Stay outside,' I say to Susan. Gingerly, I untie the bag, wrapped up as it is, like someone would tie up garden waste. Reaching inside, I can feel some hair and cold skin. With one arm, untying it wasn't easy. I had to use my knee to hold it. But to take out something from a bag is even harder unless you simply tip it out. So, I hold the bag up and something thuds out in the dark. I shine my flashlight on it, expecting to see the face of our judge. But this isn't. As best as I can tell from photographs I've seen, this is the face of Angus Porterfield.

Chapter 9

I can tell Susan has stuck her head in to see what I'm unveiling, which is something she really shouldn't have done. I can hear the tears and the words of, 'Oh my God,' as she steps away. I'd like to say I can quickly tie up the bag and close everything up again but quick is hard when you've got one hand. Ideally, I would have liked to her to help me but given the state of the poor girl, it isn't really going to happen.

When I've completed putting the body back to the way it was, albeit in various bits and pieces, I lock up the shed. I turn my attention to Susan who's sitting down and crying into her hands. She's physically shaking so I sit down with her and quickly wrap an arm around her. She shrugs me off.

'What is all this?' She says, 'What is it? I thought you were just a golfer. And I thought this was all exciting, but now people are dead. I played golf with him . . . he's dead.'

There's not a lot you can tell someone at this time except urge them to stay calm. What I do know is that I need to get her away from here, make sure she's calm and then not liable to do anything daft before I leave her. I might be seeming a bit cruel at this time, especially given the way I've been talking about her, but from a business point of view, she can't blurt this out. I need someone to find this place and find it on their own. Then another thought goes through my mind. My main purpose here is to find the judge. Where has Russell Hadleigh gone? If this body's found prematurely, that could all go up in smoke. So maybe I won't tell anybody about it, yet. I take Susan's hand and lead her away. She continues to shake and sniff along the path, back to where we'd parked her car.

I need to get her doing something normal, so when we get to her car, I tell her to drive us, not into town, but up the coast a little bit until we find a chip shop. Leaving her in the car while I pick up some fish and chips, we then head off to a beach.

Down in this part of the west side of Scotland, there's some quite long beaches, many with that pebbly sort of sand and we sit out beyond the car, eating our fish and chips. I haven't said much to her, just trying to get her something inside her stomach. Then taking her hand, we walk along, looking at the beaches, the sunsets. To other people, it might look quite romantic, but she's shaking. As we reach one end of the beach, we have to disappear behind a rock where she throws up. Strangely enough, after this, she actually seems better. Not over it, just better.

'Have you ever seen anything like that before, Paddy?' she says to me, almost as an accusation. I think about giving her the party line of, 'It's a new one on me,' but my calmness in the face of it may not substantiate the lie.

'Yes, I have, both when I was in the force and since afterwards, but you saw what was happening and that's why you have to keep quiet. You have to let me deal with this.'

'But what do I do? I mean, what do I do, having seen that?'

'You go home, because if you open your mouth about this, they'll find you and they'll terminate you, quick and simple. There's something going on here. Something that's linking back towards Russia, to a lot of people you don't want the messing about with. So, at the moment, you know nothing, you say nothing and you go on as normal. You go back to bed tonight, you sleep, you get up in the morning, you go up to the golf club, and you do the work you normally do. You play a round like you normally do.'

'Will you come to see me?'

'Of course, I will.' And actually I will, I need to make sure she's holding up. The last thing I need is her blurting something out and I've got people coming after me that I don't know about. At the moment, I think we're good; the people have the idea we're having an affair, which is fine by me. I don't mind the looks and the comments as long as they're not coming after me with guns and knives. It's nine o'clock when I drop her home; her sister's at the door, looking a little worried when she sees me with her. Kirsten waits until I'm across the road, back at my car which Susan took me to recover at the club and I tailed her home.

Susan's done remarkably well. The tears are gone, her face is cleaned up, but sisters can spot something and so Kirsten's over at my car.

'Nice to see you again. Mr. Smythe.'

'And you, Kirsten,' I say. 'How are things?'

But then her face takes on a serious tone. 'I don't care if you're messing about with my sister,' she says. 'But she takes things very sensitively. So, don't mess her about or I'll come for you.'

I could react quite strongly to this, but instead I put my hands up. 'I haven't done nothing and I don't intend to. She's a good golfer, she's a nice girl. We're just having an enjoyable time. You don't have to worry.'

'Good,' says Kirsten. 'Don't just take her and leave her. If you're interested, be extremely interested.' With that, she turns on her heel, her red hair swinging round behind and rushes back to the house. I find her attitude and her protectiveness of her sister quite appealing and she's gone up in my world. Sometimes siblings can be jealous, but there's no jealousy there. Maybe she's not interested in a man twice her age. This makes me chuckle as I pull the car away from the curb. I start to think about what's coming up.

As per normal, I park the car a couple of streets away from the Hadleigh's house, route my way in from the back, climbing over the fence. As I steal in through the kitchen, Alison Hadleigh jumps up. She's in her dressing gown again, and although this is not unusual for nearly ten o'clock at night, my arrival certainly seemed to shock her.

'It's you, is it, Mr Smythe?' Mr Smythe is it, now? She's obviously going cool on me. 'Do you have anything to show for the money I'm paying you?'

'I think we're getting somewhere. Your husband's business partners certainly didn't seem to be very happy with him. I take it you haven't heard anything yourself?' She shakes her head, turns away and asks if I want coffee. I nod, and as she makes it in the kitchen, I make my way into the front lounge, opening the curtains slightly. And there he is, parked in a different car tonight but John Carson's out there. I quickly close the curtain and decide not to let Alison know what I know in case she's wondering what I've been doing in the front room. I make it back into the kitchen by the time she pours the coffee. Her attitude seems to have changed somewhat and she sits up on the kitchen stool, her gown revealing some leg. Suddenly we're on first name terms again.

'So, Paddy, tell me all.'

'I think your husband has had business connections into the Juno brand of shops. Well, that we know, but I think he's more deeply involved than you think. My guess is he was a major part of it, if somewhat silent, but Juno isn't all it's cracked up to be. I think where their stock is coming from is dodgy.'

At this time, I don't want to give away the Russian links, because I'm not sure where Alison sits in all this. So, I decide to go with a slightly different story, one that's backed up by what I find in the offices. 'It seems,' I say, 'that the goods coming from Africa and other parts of the Third World are not coming from such ethical sources as they're reporting. I think if it becomes common knowledge, there will be a reaction and he could find his entire empire crashing down around him and that for your husband would suggest a significant loss of salary. How much do you know about his financial affairs?'

'We have separate accounts. There's a joint one for the house, which we both pay into but I have my own money, so it's not bothering me if he loses out. I just want to know where he is.'

'Yes, it does seem strange,' I say. 'He may be disappearing off to other continents, trying to sort out these supply issues, but why not just tell you he's going on a trip? It does seem somewhat bizarre, but at the moment, I think he's alive.'

She tries to show a sense of relief, but I'm not buying it. Instead, her first question is somewhat strange. 'And when do you think he will return?'

'Having not traced him,' I say, 'I couldn't tell.'

'Is it going to be before this weekend?'

'Again,' I say, 'I don't know. I'm still tracking him down. Once I find him, I'll ask him.' Except I won't be asking him because part of me thinks he's dead. It's a hunch, but I think he's mixed up in this business with the Russians. Things are going sour and they're taking out some of the parties calling the shots, putting control back to someone they know they can trust, namely Laura Sutherland, but we'll have to wait and see just how far that pans out.

'That's all remarkably interesting, Paddy. Hopefully, you'll find him soon. As for now, I'm heading off to bed, maybe for a shower first. What about yourself?'

I gave her a cheeky smile. 'I'll pass on the shower thanks; I'm sure you can scrub your own back.'

Normally people would say I wasn't offering but she doesn't. In fact, she whispers the word, 'Pity', as she walks out of the kitchen. Part of me thinks that she's now off upstairs to signal to the man outside that she's not available tonight. So, I throw her a lifeline.

'In fact, I have to go out. Most sleuthing doesn't get done during the day.' This is in fact not completely accurate, but it is a generally held belief and so I play on it. Instead, I'm going to spend the next couple of hours in a bush watching a house. 'Thanks for the coffee. You might hear me come back in tonight, you might not, depends where things lead, but I don't think I'll be back before four.'

'Four o'clock?' she says, 'You're going to be watching somebody until four o'clock?'

I nod in my head. 'Yes, definitely four, possibly five, but I don't think you'll see me before four.'

And with that, I head out the back door disappearing over the fence at the back. As soon as I've climbed over it, I pop my head up, watching. I see her at the kitchen window looking out after me. I sneak along the house beside and in darkness, I run along through some of their flower plants until I get an angle where I can see the front of Alison's house. She's up at the top bedroom window. For some reason, she's trying on a scarf. This causes John Carson to step out of his car and walk up towards the house. Everything on the ground floor is in darkness, the door opens quickly, and he disappears inside.

I'm a little bit concerned about what this relationship actually is. Why is she wanting me to look out for her husband who's off the scene when she has this fancy man coming around? He's obviously more than just a concerned friend and I don't think her husband's put him there to keep an eye on her. And if he has, he's going to be more than a little shocked by just how close and intimate he is.

I remove myself from the next-door neighbour's garden, jump into the front of Alison's garden, making my way around to the back of the house. She's locked the door, but that's not a problem. The alarm's not on and so I can enter in quite happily. I have to hide my shoes because they're mucky, covered in soil. After sticking them inside the downstairs cupboard, I make my way stealthily round to the stairs. There are voices up top and Alison seems to be talking to him about the possibilities of where her husband is. I sneak up the stairs and steal myself into a side bedroom. It's not long before I hear Alison head off for that shower, but she doesn't go alone.

I tend to think of this as the unglamorous side of what I do, having to listen to people in their hours of excitement, be that in the shower or in the bedroom that follows, trying to pick up on the odd whispered word that might actually have some relevance to the case can be rather depressing. Especially when you're a single man yourself. After a couple of hours of bouts of excitement and then rest, I was sitting in the darkness of Alison's bedroom, a conversation going on.

'Are you okay for Saturday?' says Alison, 'They're coming up, bringing a whole busload of them. It could be quite interesting.'

'Where are they holding it?'

'Out by Roger's barn. The one he's got done up, you know, the disco lights, everything. Plenty of other things too. He says he's restocked, put a few more interesting things in. I'm sure it's something you'll like.'

There's a laugh. 'Things that I'd like? I wasn't the one that got us into this. I wasn't the one that decided we needed friends.'

Some of the cryptic conversation continues and every now and then, they embrace. Frankly, I'm getting very fed up. So, I sneak back out, exit the house, and realise it's half past two. I make my way around to his car. It's not so easy to break into this one, it's quite modern, it's got all the alarms, but I get a pen light and started looking inside it.

It's a standard hire car and I can't find anything. If I wanted to, I could go back in, try and steal his keys from inside the room, which is risky enough and then have a look inside the car, but if I'm honest, there's not a lot of point. It's quite high risk for what I could find out and I doubt he's actually brought anything with him because if he had, it would be for his meeting and he would have come in with it. So instead, I stay outside until I see him leaving at about a quarter past three. There's no quick embrace on the doorstep. He simply leaves. Once his car's gone, I take a little bit of a walk, trying to have a think before routing back in to the house at about half past four in the morning. As I make my way up for landing and across to my own bedroom, the light comes on and out steps Alison Hadleigh.

'A good night's sleuthing was it?' she asks.

'Not much,' I say, 'bit of a waste of time, but that's what

happens. You end up being sore, tired, and with not a lot more on your hands. Still, back at it tomorrow.'

'You look like you could do with picking up, or a nice rub down. I'm quite good with my hands, Paddy. You're more than welcome.' And with that, she steps aside, showing me the door of her room.

The woman must be insatiable. I try not to think about counting how many times she was at it that night, but I realize that I do need sleep, and that I'm not that attracted. I'm just a single man going through the usual thing of having his dinner laid out in front of him, but not being able to eat it.

'If it's all the same to you, I try not to mix business and pleasure.'

She nods before stepping forward, and placing her hand upon my cheek. 'If you change your mind, Paddy, you don't have to knock.' She turns around, walks back into her bedroom. The door closes and as I retreat to mine, the door opens again and this time, the dressing gown's hung off, leaving very little to show. 'Remember, you don't have to knock.'

I nod, step quickly inside my room and close the door. I wonder what's up with her. Is she trying to get information out of me? Because at the end of the day, that's what I'm meant to do, be paid and give information. For some reason, does she think I'm working for somebody else, or is there some other agenda going on here? I don't care and instead, change into my boxers and climb into bed. I try to get to sleep because I am physically shattered, but in my head, I don't see Alison Hadleigh. Instead I see Susan and how upset she was. I really shouldn't have got her involved in all this, but then again, I didn't, she tailed me with a car. But I worry about where she's going in all of this. I decide to try and keep her out of it as much as possible.

Chapter 10

I manage to nod off until about ten o'clock, when my phone wakes me. It beeps, I roll over, and take a look at the message awaiting me. It tells me that my dry cleaning's ready and that they'll drop it off in person, which is nice of them. It also asks where I want it delivered. I message back, stating I'd like us to meet at the beach where I was the previous night with Susan. It was quiet and also had lots of remote spots, so it sounds perfect for dry cleaning.

I take a shower and as I step out there's Alison Hadleigh still in her dressing gown, acting like she's going to go for her own shower. 'I hope you got everything clean,' she says. 'Russell always said I was good at scrubbing his back. His front too.' The woman is unbelievable. So overt. I just say no, that I'm fine, and I need to get going. I don't; I could quite happily sit for a couple of hours having a quiet breakfast, maybe having a doze before I head out, but I reckon I'll get harassed.

As I sit in the car, thinking about where I'm going to go, Alison Hadleigh's reaction to me is bothering me. I'm not some sort of Adonis. I'm not someone you look at and think, do you know what, I wouldn't mind him in my bed for a couple of hours. Maybe it's the arm, maybe it's a weird fetish about that, but the woman just seems ravenous. John Carson was with her for how long and I'm thinking I might have to do a bit of a check on my employer, see where she goes during a day. I've got some dry cleaning to pick up, but that won't be ready until about midday. So instead I decided to pay a quick call on Susan. By this time in the morning, she should be up at the golf club, working in the pro shop. So I decide to make it a casual visit, popping up first to the restaurant. As I walk past the bar area, Kirsten's already there, and she waves me over.

'Good morning, Paddy. Is this just a social visit? Susan's working down in the pro shop.'

'In all honesty,' I say, 'I'm just needing some breakfast and I thought the food in here the other day was quite good. Why don't you join me for some?' I draw closer to Kirsten. 'I got a feeling last night that you're worried about your wee sister. My intentions are purely honourable,' I say. I do realize that actually that's the sort of thing people say when they're not.

'I'm sure she can look after herself, but by all means let's have breakfast.' As the morning's quite bright, Kirsten suggests that we sit outside with a view over the eighteenth hole. I have my eggs, bacon and some toast, but she sits with a bowl of granola. She's at that age in life where it's not difficult to look good, not difficult to be in shape. Pointless eating broken biscuits if you ask me. When she asks what I think of her sister, I get the feeling that I'm being interrogated.

'Your sister's lovely, she's got a heck of a golf game, and she's a lot of fun, but don't worry. I'm not going to sleep with her.' In an older generation, that sort of statement would have shocked, but Kirsten simply says, 'It's up to you, whether you do or not. But if you do, don't make it a quick one-off fling, make sure there's a possibility at the end of it for something more. There are rumours going about—people have seen you.

So, I don't want my sister dragged through that. She's not some sort of little tart. Neither of us are. I don't want her given that, that name. Cause you'll move on and she'll end up just being the thing that anybody else can play with.'

I lean forward taking my one hand and grabbing hold of Kirsten's. 'Don't worry,' I say, 'she's too nice a person to do that to. But she is a little bit taken with me and yes, that's enjoyable, but she's too young.'

Kirsten smiles. 'Keep it that way. Susan's a good judge of character normally, can usually see if somebody's half decent or not. Unlike me—I pick the wrong ones.'

'Can I ask you something,' I say, 'kind of off the record.' She nods. 'I bumped into Alison Hadleigh the other day and she was quite a forthcoming woman, actually made a pass at me.'

I see Kirsten's face. She's starting to laugh. 'Yes, she's quite the forward woman. A lot of rumours around her, a lot of rumours around her and the judge. I'd watch yourself. Well, unless it's a quick fling you're looking for; she's a bit of a man-eater apparently. A lot of other rumours.' And then her face goes quite solemn, 'Yeah. A lot of other rumours.'

I decide that's something worth exploring. 'Did you know her personally? Have you had experience?' And then I see the fire come in the eyes.

'I've had experience. My ex-boyfriend, she played around with him behind my back. He wasn't a bad sort either, but she entranced him, and she took him, he said, to places that, well, you know how you guys speak?' I try to probe further, but she clams up, telling me she needs to get back to work.

'Sorry,' I say, 'if I brought up something you didn't want to think about.'

I drop in to the pro shop to see Susan. She's laying out some stock and she's giving me quite a cool look. I ask how she is and she says, 'Fine.' I ask if she's going out to play a round today. She says, 'Yes, the pro's joining me.'

I think that's a good thing because the last thing I need is her snooping around the twelfth. I tell her I'll maybe see her tonight. At which point she looks at me quite coldly before smiling. 'Yeah,' she says, 'tonight, let's get something tonight.' And with that she disappears off. I'll need to keep an eye on her; she seems particularly shaken. At the end of the day, the poor girl's only eighteen. You don't want to see that thing at any age.

Conversation complete, I jump in my car and head off up the coast to find the beach where my dry cleaning is going to be. I'm sitting in the car looking out to the sea when there's a tap on the window. I turn my head, but the person that did it is walking away. I give a smile because I know who it is.

Martha Harris was a particularly clever woman. Unfortunately, that cleverness meant that she got caught up in a particularly bad finance scam, being one of the people at the centre of it. Although not the mastermind, but certainly the person with the brains to carry it out, Martha was led down the garden path by the guy who was running it with promises of marriage. He happily reinforced that idea every night, by taking her to bed, but they managed to get put him away for a number of years. Martha, on the other hand, although the actual brains, appeared not be involved to any serious degree and was seen as very much a victim. She was a victim of the heart maybe, but she certainly knew what she was doing, though she was doing it for the wrong man. That's when Martha came to work for me.

She's a wiz. She can track anything down, can get into

accounts of anywhere. She's what you need when you're no longer in the police force with access to lots of things. But she's also rather a sad figure. She took it hard when she realized he was playing her along the whole time. Back in the day, Martha was never slim. She was curvy with a little bit of weight on, but now she's excessively overweight and that's come from the pain. It's quite sad when you see her, but you can tell it's her as she usually dresses in long black cardigans, white skirts. She looks like she's in mourning the whole time. And frankly she is. She keeps her hair long because that was how he liked it. And she wears a pair of thick-rimmed glasses. I like Martha, but she's a hell of a tragic figure.

She's waiting for me on a bench that overlooks the beach and I sit down beside her. Handing me a small USB stick, she says, 'It's all on there, Paddy.'

I nod. 'Thanks, Martha. How are you doing?'

She turns to look at me, 'It's been a year without a drink, a year without a drink, Paddy.'

'That's good, Martha. That's really good.'

'I suppose. Thanks to you, keeping busy. Something to keep my mind off it. Can't stop eating though. Just want to eat sometimes, nothing else.'

'You should get out more. See people.'

She turns her head away. 'That's what they all say. How do you see people when you look like this?' I think about turning around and giving her the thing of getting back into shape and feeling better and more comfortable with the right people, but the woman's got a depression that comes deep from within, and I'm no counsellor. People always want to offer advice, but really you should only give it when you know it's good advice. When you're some sort of expert, or lived it yourself, even then, you should be careful with advice.

'Did I ever tell you I thought about offices?' I say. 'If I do that, you can come in and work day to day in an office. You might not see much of me, but you'll see the other staff.'

She laughs. 'You'll never have an office, Paddy. You work too much on the dark side and you wouldn't want it. I'll be a smiling face for the public coming in to book your services? That's not you.'

'No, I guess not,' I say, 'but maybe I'll get a receptionist. Anyway, what's the story?'

'This company, Juno, there's something nasty going around with it. I tried to trace all those links to Africa, but it's not there. When you go back to where these companies say their supplies are coming from, the links end up back in Eastern Europe. There's lots of dummy companies floating around, a lot of Russian gangster and tell-tale signs over the lot of it. You need to be careful, Paddy; that's the kind of people that don't usually mess about. They're also not just into running clothing—that seems to be a smaller part of the operation. Something to keep the funding coming in. I tried tracing the companies back and they get down to Eastern Europe and a large number of different factories. There're rumours from certain reports I've had access to, that these are sweatshops, but there's nothing confirmed. There's been raids into places by local authorities, but everything's gone by the time they get there. But each time the reports say, trafficking and sweat shops. Not really the image that Juno is purporting, is it?'

'Not really, Martha,' I say. 'Any way of tracing this money back and presenting it?"

"Not easy," she says, "There's a lot of rumour. Trying to get fixed transactions isn't happening, the dummy companies are good, and I could take a bit of a punt with several of them, but some of the links are tenuous. They're there, just not provable. I haven't got a full trail, Paddy, sorry. I'll keep working on it."

"Thanks Martha, but no stupid risks. Make sure they can't trace it back if it's like this. The last thing I need is you getting a visit.'

She nods. 'Don't worry—you know I'm good at this thing. Do you think I could play volleyball?' she says suddenly.

'Volleyball. Why not?'

'You know why not, Paddy, look at the size of me.'

'Doesn't mean you can't stand there and hit a ball with your wrists. Be good for you. Maybe one day you'll get up to playing at beach volleyball.'

She laughs. 'I think my pants are disappearing up my arse as it is.' And then she becomes melancholy again.

'Go and play your volleyball. Is it mixed?'

'Yes,' she says, 'it's just a little church group. There's a couple of nice people in it. I thought it might get me out the door.'

'Then do it. Next time tell me how it goes. Don't worry if you're crap at it; it's not about being good at it. That might help keep you off the bottle even longer. A year, Martha, that's bloody good. You still at the meeting?'

'Every week,' she says, 'every week.'

'I'll take a scan through this you've given me; otherwise, stay safe. See what else you can dig up for me.' Martha nods, stands up awkwardly, starts to walk away. The day's not particularly warm. It's pleasant, not warm. But Martha's sweating as she walks. A lot of people would look at her and just judge her for what she is now, and to be honest, she's a bit of a wreck. She was quite something in her day. She had a personality that attracted. Yeah, she was shy, but she could speak, and she was intelligent. And yes, she had looks. Now, I just feel for her. I watch her walk across the car park, get into an old red Fiat Panda. Even her car's depressing.

As I sit and watch the waves in front of me, I wonder what else I should do today. Finding and tailing Sergei could be tough. So, I might go after Laura Sutherland, find out what's going on. They were together. It's then that my mobile phone starts ringing, and I see the number; it's Susan. I pick it up and she's in a bit of a flap.

'Calm down,' I say, 'I'm struggling to make sense of you. Where are you?'

'I'm inside the women's toilets. Trying to be quiet, but you're not going to believe it, Paddy. Paddy, you won't believe it!'

'What's wrong?'

'It's gone. It's gone; it's been taken down and it's gone. There's just like a concrete base there.'

'What has?' I say.

'The shed, Paddy. I went out golfing today. We got to the twelfth and I'm looking, and the shed's not there. The shed wasn't where it was. I mean, it was there last night, Paddy. Am I going mad? It was there, wasn't it? With, you know, inside?'

'Yes, it was,' I say. 'Have you asked anybody about it? Have you spoken, just sort of pointed out the fact that where the hell's the shed?'

'I mentioned it when I got back inside,' she said, 'but that was the thing that really got me. I was talking to the pro, and he said that it came down from the club secretary, Angus Porterfield. Paddy, he said it came from Angus Porterfield. How could it come from Angus Porterfield? He was cut up in there. He was bloody well cut up!' And with that she starts to cry, sobbing heavily. It's not good, her being in such a state. I don't know if she's going to be able to hold it together.

'Take it easy. Okay, calm yourself. Go wash your face in the sink, then go tell your boss you're having a few issues. When he asks what, tell him it's female things, because we won't have a clue what to do, us men. That will get you the afternoon off. Go home. I'll pick you up. Okay? And we'll sort this out.'

She murmurs, 'Okay.' But then I hear her cry more. 'Angus Porterfield, he was in bits, how does he speak when he's been in bits, Paddy?' But I'm up on my feet already moving to my car. I just reiterate to her, 'Calm down, face wash, tell boss you're going home, not well. Go home. I'll pick you up. Nothing else. Just focus on those. And then we go from there.' It may seem harsh, but I switch off the phone. If I stay on the line, her senses keep feeding to me, keep bubbling over again. And she's not in a secure place to do that. But I realize I need to get to her quick, because the last thing I need is her babbling anything out.

Chapter 11

I reckon it will take Susan about half an hour to get home. So, I stop off, pick up a few drinks and things to eat, and pop them in the boot before heading round. When I knock on the door, she opens it and almost collapses on me, flopping as if everything has just ended. I catch her. It's awkward with one arm, but I move her back inside the house, kicking the door closed behind me. I'm not sure who's in. Her sister will probably be working. Even after all this time, I'm not sure who she lives with.

'Anyone in?' I ask.

'No. Mum's at her work.'

'And your father?' I say.

'He left some time ago. I was small when he left her.' Then, she sniffs, lifting her head. 'But they moved it. They moved the whole thing.'

'I know,' I say. 'Well, that's not our problem. What you need to be doing is staying quiet.'

'But, Paddy,' she says, her shoulders shaking, arms clenching. 'Shouldn't we just take all this to the police? I mean, he was dead in there. His head was lobbed off.' She begins to cry again. I reach forward, putting my arm around the shoulder.

'If it were that simple, I would. But, you need to understand, there's somebody else still missing, and if he's alive then going to the police may put him in jeopardy. There's also the question of the farm. That's why I haven't moved on it. There's also no real evidence except what we saw and heard. If they don't bring anybody to the farm, it's unlikely the police could do much with it. Sometimes, you have to pick your time, Susan.'

It's not very comforting, and she continues to sniff and cry. I rustle her hair with my hand. She pulls herself close, leaning her head upon my chest. I'm not sure if that was the appropriate action I was looking for. It's quite hard to comfort somebody without giving them physical contact, but with her interest in me and not wanting to make it increase, it's difficult to show compassion. But, what the hell? She needs a shoulder to cry on at the moment, not some aloof idiot.

'I think it's time you and I went out,' I say to her. Sitting in her front room, the TV in one corner, there are pictures of her golfing triumphs on the mantelpiece. It could be too easy a place to remind her of how her perfectly ideal world is falling apart. So, instead she needs to get out, and she needs to be doing something. 'Go and get a change of clothing,' I say. 'Something older. What size is your mum compared to you?'

'We're not far different,' she says.

'Good. Get something old or something you normally wouldn't wear. Put that on. Some trousers as well, and we'll drop by somewhere. Change your hair colour.'

That gave her a shock. She looks at me, almost resentful. 'No,' I say, 'not permanently. We'll just get you a wig. But, get something to tie the hair up as well. You'll need to pin it down underneath the wig.'

I decide to go and check up on my employer, work out what's happening with her. I also want to try and trace Laura or Sergei and what's going on there. That could be difficult. I want to see how Susan operates with something less dangerous. At the moment, my belief is Alison will be an easier target. I'm not quite sure how she fits into the whole scheme of things, but there's definitely something strange going on, and John Carson seems to be far too close for a woman who's saying she's missing her husband. There's always a possibility she's involved, but why call in a private investigator just to show . . . what? Some sort of idea that she wasn't involved? I'm that incompetent, she thinks I'd find nothing?

Ten minutes later, Susan comes downstairs, her red hair still hanging behind her head. She's wearing a blazer that looks like something you would wear in an office, a pair of slacks that are black, and some heels underneath. It suits her and gives her a more mature look, which honestly is a bit of a problem for me, because so far in my head, I have been telling myself she is way too young. With this older look, it makes keeping my distance a bit harder. But, don't worry. I will. She still is too young.

I send her back upstairs to get a pair of Plimsoles, or something without heels, just in case we have to run, although, to be honest, the heels look nice. Susan returns, we get in the car, and we drive off. I ask her if they have a dressing up shop, or something akin, dressing up outfits. She points me to an all-in-one card and gift shop which looks the business. There's a vampiress outfit. It has a wig attached to it and looks fairly substantial. I purchase it, go back to the car, and ask her to throw it on. It's not perfect, looking a little bit distressed, but I'd say it was her hair if I didn't know better. Her hand comes across, touches my knee.

'I'm sorry, Paddy. I'm not good at this. You must think me

an idiot.'

I shake my head. That's when I notice that the green eyes with the black hair doesn't really suit, but it'll have to do. 'You know, Susan,' I say, 'it's just as I get older and I see more of this, I get less shocked by it. If you weren't upset by it, I'd be pretty worried.' That seems to strengthen her. Her hand's still on my knee, and I gently remove it. 'We have work to do. Let's take your car and see if we can find Alison.'

So, we swap cars and drive off to Alison's house, driving past the front. Her car is still there. As we pass by, I see her in one of the windows, prancing about. I get Susan to park slightly off the street, and we sit waiting.

'Why don't we get out and do something?' says Susan. I see her still trembling.

'No,' I say. 'She's going to leave soon. This happens a lot in my business. You sit and wait. You have to get used to it.' I reach into the back, pull out packet of crisps, opening them and placing them in front of her. 'Smokey bacon,' I say. 'Go ahead.' She devours the crisps, and I reckon it's because she needs something to do. But, it's as she's putting her hand in for the last few crumbs, I see a car departing behind me. It's Alison, the bright red car pulling away in front of us. Susan jumps to follow her. I hold her shoulder. 'Just hold a second. Just a second. Now, pull out.'

Now that we're doing something, Susan seems to have settled with less shakes. She's intent, focused, which is what my intention has been all along. She's too keen with the car though and I have to keep reminding her to hold back, especially as Alison heads out of town. She pulls off into the car park which I remember.

'It belongs to the sports centre where we first met,' I tell

Susan, indicating that she pull up and wait. I see Alison stepping out of her car and making her way over to the centre. She's wearing a beige pair of trousers, and the blouse is open, at least the top three buttons. She's giving me that impression she's out to allure someone. The hair, neatly manicured, face made up, and wearing a heel that almost makes her feet go vertical. 'Go to the car and then go into the reception,' I say to Susan. 'If needs be, start looking at some brochures or something. I'll be in a couple of minutes. Just to keep an eye on where Alison moves to. Okay?'

Susan nods and races out of the car, making me wonder if she's got an appetite for this type of work. When she's gone, I step out and look into the boot of my car. Attaching a beard, I put the prosthetic arm on and change into a shirt to cover it. It can be awkward doing this and may not look ideal. So, I throw on some glasses as well, and a wig of my own. Still being the morning, there are not that many members about. I hope my disguise is good as I walk in the front door. Having been there not that long ago, I recognize the receptionist in the front desk, but she gives me no inkling, no eyebrows raised. Susan actually looks at me before she suddenly smiles. I'll have to watch and keep her in check. I walk up, take her by the hand, and march off into the facility. Turning over to pretend to peck her on the cheek, I whisper, 'Where'd she go?'

Susan doesn't answer. She simply takes my hand, pulling me along, and I soon spot the long, blonde hair of Alison Hadleigh. She is sitting in the cafe with a man in front of her. He's reasonably stocky, younger than her, I would say, maybe late twenties, early thirties, but she certainly seems to be captivating him. He's like some sort of hungry dog with her, hanging on every word. We walk past, moving into another part of the building before I stop, turn around, and start looking through the glass pan of some doors, watching their conversation. They seem to be talking about what they want. Alison shakes her head, steps up, and moves off in the direction of the food counter. So, I grab Susan, telling her when I sit down, she needs to strike up a convincing conversation with me.

We quickly hurry to the table next to Alison and her new man. When we sit down, Susan asks me in a gentle voice if I want something to drink. I reach over with my hand, holding hers and say, 'Yes,' asking for a coffee, but then start up some sort of conversation. We're talking about moving house. I start mentioning has Susan seen any of the places, and she falls into step almost perfectly. When I hear Alison sit down behind us, I let go of Susan's hand, indicating she should go up and get the coffees. With Susan up getting the coffee, I get a chance to listen in. Alison and her friend, apparently called Dominic, seem to be discussing a guest list of some sort. There's talk of people in town, some coming from afar, and one international person, at least. Whatever it is, it's happening this Saturday. Then, there's talk of a venue.

Susan sits down in front of me, and I have to prompt her to start talking. It's quite an art to talk and listen at the same time, and I doubt Susan will be able to do it, but as long as she talks to me, it will keep up the pretence. From the odd snippet I hear, it's quite clear it's going to be a reasonable gathering. There's at least twenty people mentioned. There's talk of moving it to a different hotel because, apparently, the owner will be coming along as well, and his bookings for this week have fallen through. I catch the name. It's a Mr Laurel, Matthew Laurel to be precise, although Dominic seemed to call him Matt. Apparently, it's not Matthew's first time to throw something like this. Alison's asking how they're going to get the equipment there, but, Dominic has a van, and he'll happily pop around anytime. That's about the substance of the conversation, and lots of names that are hard to remember because they're all first names. There's no description really with it. There was a brief mention of Dominic's partner, but she's not coming. Dominic's also been given charge of organizing the games, whatever that means.

The meeting's over fairly abruptly, but Dominique offers to walk Alison out to her car. She gets up with him in tow like a Labrador puppy. I have to put my hand forward, stopping Susan from standing. Once I'm sure Alison and Dominic have moved far enough away, I lean over and tell Susan to stay there and don't move. She asks why, and I tell her that she's providing cover for me, somewhere to come back to while I go off to ask a question at reception. Satisfied with my answer, Susan sits there and looks around, staring at the various courts around us.

I stride off, get to reception as I see the two we've been listening to out in the car park, beside Alison's red car. It's there I see them touch for the first time. They look around each other, trying to see if anyone's about. There clearly isn't because there follows an embrace. It was passionate, probably more hungry than passionate. It didn't look like lovers. It looked like something else. Who is this woman that's employed me? A part of me thinks there can't be much between her and her husband if this is going on. That's at least two men she's been with. But this guy is a lot younger. Maybe she has needs that aren't being satisfied. It's not my sort of case, really.

I wonder how her husband would react if he found out. I

watch the red car drive off as I'm asking the receptionist about their fees. She hands me the leaflet she handed me several days ago, but it's not her fault. This disguise is quite good, especially when you drop the Ulster accent. I head back to pick up Susan. Once we get to her car, sitting in front, she turns and smiles at me. 'That was fun, Paddy. Is this what you do all the time, listening in, sneaking around?' I shake my head.

'No, not all the time. A lot of hard graft goes on. A lot of boring pouring over figures and facts.'

'Do you need a partner?' she asks.

'I've got plenty of partners. I've got people that do different aspects of my job for me.'

'Yeah, but you need someone out and about with you.' I check her face, and it's not just infatuation. She seems to actually have a hunger for this. Her shoulders are forward, the teeth are beaming and it's almost like she's begging me to let her join in. This is becoming a hard call. If I piss her off at this point, she may go back into that melancholy about what she's seen. At the moment, her eyes are being taken off it. I have to say that she functioned brilliantly in the cafe. Almost a natural.

'Did you hear much in that cafe while you were talking to me?' I ask.

'It wasn't easy. You were talking to me. I was talking to you.'

'Yes, I know,' I say. 'Tell me what you heard.' We sit for five minutes. She rattles off several names that I'd forgotten. Did she pick up everything important? Probably about 95%. As I listen, going through my head is the question about what this will do to the relationship between ourselves. Maybe it could be good. Maybe it could formalize it more. Maybe she could see me as a boss and not some older man she wants to flirt with.

After imparting all the information, she sits sideways in the driver's seat, leaning forward to me. 'What about it, Paddy?'

When we're talking about the likes of Alison Hadleigh, I'm extremely comfortable about what Susan is doing, but if things go wrong, it's no bad shakes. Might lose my wages, but hey, I could handle that. I could probably even talk my way out of it. But, with the Russian mob, things might be different.

'Okay, Susan,' I say. 'I'll take you on, but you've got to listen, and you've got to learn. If I say go home, you go home. There are certain parts of this I don't want you being seen around. Okay? You can stay with me the rest of the day. Tomorrow, it's back to the golf club.'

She smiles and leans forward to give me a peck on the cheek.

'That has to stop,' I say. 'Whatever it is you're feeling for me in that way, I am now your boss, and that's where it sits. That's the deal because you can't feel like that and do this job.' She leans back suddenly. I can see her eyes darting this way and that. Then, she says something incredibly upfront. 'It was really a pipe dream between me and you, Paddy, wasn't it? You're probably enjoying driving around with me, me with you, but it wasn't going to go anywhere in that sense.'

I shake my head. 'So, are you in?'

She looks at me with that strange, dark hair that really doesn't suit her after seeing the bright red hair, her natural hue. 'You said I don't have to go back to work until tomorrow. So, where are we off, Paddy? Where next?'

Chapter 12

MatthewI'm not sure how impressed Susan is, but my first decision is to go and get some lunch. But she listens intently as I run her through what happened this morning. I ask her does she know any of the names. And she doesn't, so I task her with two things.

Over the next half hour, I want her to find a hotel that's owned by Matthew Laurel, in the local area. And I also want an address for Laura, Laura Sutherland. The golf club should have it, and that's where I've asked Susan to start. But as she's ill, of course she can't go in.

I sit enjoying a cottage pie, with the potatoes well mashed up. It's got a nice golden crust to it and they put in enough meat to keep me satisfied. Too often cottage pies come with just gravy underneath.

As I'm wolfing this food into me, I see Susan go to pick up her phone. I ask who she's calling and she says the golf club. While sitting and finishing my meal, I listen to her as she calls up the club secretary. Correction, the club office, finding out an address for Laura Sutherland, insisting that she needs to drop off something from the pro shop to her.

She writes it down on a piece of paper and slides it over to me. Now she sits on her phone, thumbs awhirl, finding out something else for me. I take my own phone and Google the address, finding it to be on the outskirts of Stranraer.

When I next look up, Laura's adjusting her wig. It's almost like she's trying to be professional about all of this, taking on a detached air. Which is perfectly fine by me. I just have to watch she doesn't overplay things. Sometimes you try and act out the character rather than just be it.

The best disguise is always in plain sight in front of people. But she's got an address for the hotel. I say we get in the car and take a spin past and she agrees. The hotel itself is on the edge of town, just out in the country and separate to everything else.

It's not massive. From the outside, it looks like it has maybe twenty bedrooms. There's a slightly dilapidated sign in the front, with a little wooden piece that gets dropped in, presumably to change the price. It says £89 a night for a double room, which to me seems expensive, but I guess if you're stuck out here you'll pay what you pay.

It'll be three star at best, and come to that, I can't think of anything that's two star. Usually at that point they don't mention what the rating is. They just take your money and hope for the best.

I send Susan into the hotel to pick up some leaflets and find out a little bit about what goes on there. When she comes back, she advises me that it has eighteen bedrooms and they're booked up this Saturday. There's simply no room to stay on this Saturday night.

I hadn't mentioned that bit to her. She'd gone and asked that off her own bat. Maybe she does have a mind for this.

She also tells me that there was only the proprietor there. And she couldn't see anyone else moving about. Presumably, there are maids to change the beds. But she thought he looked quite alone and certainly there seemed to be no wife about.

'That's a bit of a jump,' I tell her, 'but I like your thinking.' We leave the rather drab structure, with its long windows leading straight to what in the past might've been called sunrooms, and drab curtains that sit in a line above the ground floor indicating each bedroom.

Any furniture I can see from this position also looks weary. I feel any bookings on a Saturday night would certainly help somewhere like this. But I have the feeling these are different sort of bookings.

Maybe that's why he's taking it. Maybe he's not actually involved. I don't know, but I do know that I'll probably be here on Saturday night, although in a visual capacity only. All sounds a bit much for me to partake in.

I tell Susan to head off to our next address which I realize is in the posh part of town. Alison Hadleigh's place was quite something. But it's nothing compared to this.

Laura Sutherland has a drive like at an opening first hole in a golf course. There seems to be a gardener working and her front door has two pillars either side of it. I would say there's six or seven rooms in the house.

It's like a mini-castle, with grey stone, and one corner has a turret at the top of it, while beneath are small slit windows. I'm not sure it's genuine, or if it's been built onto a more modern house. Rather, I think she's gone for the effect of trying to be the Scottish baronial home.

It looks crass. But I don't have the sort of money to try my own version. But she certainly does.

'How well do you know Laura Sutherland?' I ask Susan. 'I mean what does she does for a living?'

'You mean apart from getting involved with Russian people and bringing dodgy clothing into the country?'

A little bit of sarcasm. She's certainly warmed up from earlier on today. In fact, I believe she probably hasn't thought about that decapitated head. I'll not bring it up.

'Yes,' I say. 'Apart from that.'

'I don't really know. She seems to have fingers in a lot of pies,' says Susan. 'I do know that she brings a lot of people to the club. One-off rounds, businessmen passing through. Businesswomen too. She always strikes me as that high powered, classy woman. And I've played many a round with her because I guess they like me on show, that clever kid who can really play a bit. I think she told me once I can be quite a bit of eye candy.'

I ignore the tease. Having set the grounds of boss and employee, I'm not going to try and reengage. I like this new position, especially the way of being able to put a barrier up as an employer. She's my pupil and that's where she'll stay. But I did get her point, and I could see someone like Laura using her in that way.

'She ever ask you for anything more? You know, to stop on afterwards, enjoy a meal, head off to some house?'

'What? With some sleaze ball? Give me a break. I've got a bit more class than that. I used to enjoy if she gave me a tip or two if we played. And you could also win money on the round because they always wanted to bet. Hotshots coming in with their big clothes, but mostly couldn't play that well. They thought they could, but our course isn't that easy and I know it. I know it like the back of my hand, Paddy. I'm not easy to beat at home.'

We park further down the street and I get out. I walk

along it, checking the house for signs of occupancy. Apart from the gardener, there's a car in the side. It's a flash BMW, businesswoman's car. But beyond that, there's a convertible. I think it's a Porsche.

She's obviously someone with quite a bit of money. And she spends it well.

I pass the house twice before I notice the other car also parked up. It's black and has tinted windows, and there's someone in the front. I'm sure I've seen it before. The Russian goons were in it. Maybe they're keeping an eye on her.

I decide to walk around the back of the house. It's more of a country lane back there, the house sitting off a main road. This is no estate we're on, with neighbours to overlook and to see. Instead the rear lawns are enclosed with trees and the country lane has but one car sat in it.

It's old, maybe ten years, twelve years. A small Peugeot. There's a bit of rust on one side but no one in it and it makes me wonder why it's parked here.

I go up to the fence that guards the house. And at the back of the house I can see movement. There's a woman, brunette hair, moving about. Soon out of the back of the house comes a track-suited figure. The trainers are solid dirty grey. It's a drab outfit and there's a beanie hat on the woman. It is quite bizarre because at the moment, it's warm.

I move quickly to the edge of the house, hiding behind a hedge, and watch as she emerges through a security gate right into the lane at the back. She steps into the car and it begins to drive off. Quickly I grab my phone, ringing Susan, telling her to drive round to the lane at the back. The number plate's ringing through my head as well.

Susan comes along quickly, but not ridiculously, and I jump

in. 'Drive to the end of this road and keep going. We're looking for a Peugeot, old, blue, rust on the side.'

Susan doesn't ask why. Instead I can see her hands grip the wheel tight, shoulders go forward. This thing's really gripping her, really getting in under her skin, and I remember the feeling. In fact, I still have the feeling every now and then.

The blue car takes a left at the end of the lane. We are just about to catch it and we follow round and see it turning left again, now making its way along the road in front of her own house. I reckon Laura Sutherland's checking out the opposition, or at least her partners.

Thankfully, we're not there looking. But the black car is, and it doesn't do anything as we all drive past. She'll be happy she's lost her tail now.

I keep Laura at a distance, as we head off out of Stranraer into the countryside. We travel at least five miles, until we end up on the coast road. We're on the far side of the peninsula, away from Loch Ryan, looking into the Irish Sea. It's the bit everybody going for the ferry never gets to see, because you have to drive fast and around. A good place to be away from everything.

You don't pass through any of these places; you have to be going there. There's a little cottage on the side of the shore, and I watch Laura turn her car off up a short drive and stop. We drive past and I tell Susan to pull in as soon as she can. We must be five hundred yards down the road when she manages to get off the road and find a collection of trees to set the car behind.

I tell her to stay put and quickly get out, making my way through fields and undergrowth until I can see the house and Laura's car. I watch for a minute or two before skirting the property, keeping low in the grass.

There are not a lot of trees here, so it's hard to get close to it. But she's not in the car, so I presume she's inside. Seeing no one looking out of the windows, I run quickly up to the rear wall of the house.

It's a white cottage, maybe only three rooms. But someone's inside because there's smoke coming out of the chimney. I jump beside one of the windows and try to listen.

The wind's blowing, which is obscuring the sound, and I can hear the crashing waves on the shore. But I can also hear Laura's voice. She's saying something about those damned Russians. A man speaks back, but he's hard to make out.

Apparently, things are not to plan and they're not happy. That I know. She says something to him, but I don't hear it because I hear a *pfft*, the sort of sound that people use on the stage to indicate they're grabbing someone's attention. What it's doing out here I have no idea.

I scan around me. And then I see the black hair, or at least the false wig, of my partner. She should've stayed put and I'm going to need to have a strong word with her. But where she is now is not a good place to be.

I step back away from the window, trying to look in. Yes, the two voices are definitely coming from this room, so I wave her away from me, telling her to move round to the edge and then come up the side of the house, towards me.

She's got that fitness of youth and she's able to run with bent knees, down low. She quickly moves up beside me and whispers in my ear, 'What's going on?'

To which I turn round and whisper back, 'You're out of line. You should be in the car.' Her face looks crestfallen. But I don't care. It's true.

I hold my finger up to my lips and try and listen in again. But I don't hear anything. It seems they've moved. And so, I start to sneak round.

As I reach the corner of the house, I realize that two people have exited it and are now standing in the drive. I see Laura Sutherland's disguise, the faded track suit. And she's opening the boot of the car.

A stocky man reaches in and takes out a bag of groceries, moving back inside the house with Laura following him. I move back to my position below the window in the far room. I can hear him taking out various tins.

He says, 'No milk? Just this powdered crap.' Laura says something about beggars not being choosers.

I must've been crouched behind that wall for an hour, Susan beside me. And most of the conversation I'm struggling to pick up. There are long silences at times and they seem to be drinking a generous-sized bottle of wine between them.

I wouldn't say that they were cold to each other. In fact, quite the opposite. But they seemed to be people in a difficult situation. Sentences are short, but not harsh. A couple of times Laura says the phrase, 'What shall we do—how do we play this?' and 'It could mean the end of the company.'

I need to go back and check my records about who exactly stands to make out of Juno and the businesses around it. Maybe Laura's heavily involved. Maybe this other man is as well.

Susan taps my arm and I lean in. 'I think I know the voice,' she says. 'I know the man. I've heard it at the club, but it's very strained at the moment. I'm sure it's somebody I've played with.'

I have to stop her as there's movement inside. We make our

way back across to the end of the house where we see Laura and the man coming out together. Susan looks round. As soon as she does, she ducks back in again and starts tapping me on the shoulder, but I hold my hand up as I'm watching what's unfolding.

The pair come to the car, with some harsh words. But then the man roughly grabs the woman. It's not an attack, it's like an outburst of emotion. And suddenly, they're chewing the face off each other, arms running all over their bodies. It's brief, but as they step away hands are left touching.

They're looking into each other's eyes with a solemnness. It's a sad parting, but it's a parting that's loaded with something else. He says the words, 'Take care and don't trust him.'

Susan's grabbing my arm, but again I'm having to hold my hand up. As I watch Laura drive away, the man stands watching her depart. He then makes his way inside and again Susan wants to tell me something.

But instead I take her hand, move away to the side of the building, and then scoot round it back towards our car, all the time indicating to Susan she should stay quiet.

When we flop down into our seats, she turns to me with giddy excitement, looking at me. 'Did you see who that was?'

'I only saw somebody from the back,' I say.

'The dark hair. But the voice. And then I saw him,' she said. 'That's the person you're looking for.'

This hits me like a sledgehammer, because I thought he was dead. 'You don't mean?' I say.

'Yes!' she says. 'That's the judge. That's Russell Hadleigh. What the hell's he doing out here? And since when was he with Laura?'

Chapter 13

The sudden appearance of a man I thought possibly dead is a little bit off-putting. As we drive back in the car to Susan's, she keeps telling me that the judge was never seen with Laura. She just wasn't one of his crowd. John Carson was. John Carson's wife and various other people she mentions, but not Laura. I make the decision that I need to get into that house, see what the deal is with the judge. I'm not ready to talk to him personally yet, but if I can get in and see any of his computers or anything else, I might have a chance working out what's going on.

John Carson's also a man I haven't spoken to yet and with Susan mentioning his name again, it makes me think I should pop and see him. Too often he's popped round and seen Alison Hadleigh. So, what's the connection there? I had thought John possibly might have bumped off the judge, but that's clearly not true. So why does he keep coming round and bothering Alison? Why do they look like they're having some sort of an affair? And what's this large meeting that's going to happen? There's not a lot I can do about the meeting, except go to it when it's there. We know the hotel; we know where it's at. But in the meantime, I'll go and take a look at John Carson's this evening. See if I can't find a bit more out about him in his home. And then maybe in the small hours, I'll go back and see the judge.

But these sorts of things are not for Susan. She might be becoming an employee of mine, but I don't risk that sort of thing to a newbie. And after breaking of the rules, following me when I told her not to, I'm not sure I'm going to trust her on a stakeout. On the way back in the car, I point out her error, and in fairness, she's contrite. I pointed out if he'd seen her come out, her cover would've been blown. He'd wonder what she was doing there because he knows her. And then she argued that she didn't know the judge was in there. I pointed out that quite often we don't know who we're looking at—that's the whole point. If we did, we wouldn't need to go around nosing.

I think she's a little dispirited. So, I get her to stop off at a small cafe and I buy her a dinner. It seems to cheer her up. She talks enthusiastically about working for me. I'm trying to foster that big brother/little sister relationship because that's what I want her to be, and she seems to be going with it. She's grabbing hold of Paddy, leaning on Paddy, or maybe that just came from seeing her first body, especially a cut-up one. Hopefully, the initial infatuation of an older man that plays golf has dropped off. It's nine o'clock when I drop her home, pick up my own car, and head off to see John Carson.

I give Alison Hadleigh a ring, pretending to update her on what's happening. I don't mention I've seen her husband, because frankly I don't trust the woman. Instead, I tell her I'm investigating something, so I won't be back.

John Carson's address is one of many Susan's been able to get for me, and the neighbourhood he lives in is reasonably plush. The house sits on the edge of the street, but it's one of those good ones, trim lawns, everything nice and neat. Cars outside speak of people doing okay, nothing unbelievably ostentatious, but good. You know the sort. Able to possibly send their kids to a small private school, certainly able to pay for everything. Holiday every year, somewhere nice, maybe even skiing.

I stop the car some distance away and walk past the house. Pretending my shoelace is undone, I tie it up and look from the far side of the road. Night's beginning to fall. There are lights on in the house and I count three cars. Susan's never mentioned any kids with John Carson, so he may have guests. I walk past again, then just stand on the other side of the street, but much closer, enough that I see movement inside the house. Checking the rest of the street, I walk back to my car and change into a black jacket. I make sure everything I'm wearing is dark and then walk calmly across the street, before dropping into the driveway. Out of the three cars, one is smaller, a little run around. There's no BMW here but the cars are still worth a bit and they look new. Well, newish. I don't think these go for an MOT.

I've done this thing a lot, sneaking around people's houses, and this one's a cinch. As I walk around the back, I hear laughter. Peering in the window, I see four people, one of whom is John Carson. There's a rather large woman beside him, maybe in her fifties. There's a man opposite John; he's taller and more rugged and I'd say somewhere around the forty to fifty age bracket. And then there's a girl. Well, I say girl, for my age. She's maybe in her mid-twenties.

She looks like a librarian from a teenage mystery novel. She's wearing glasses, unlike the older lady, who's in an evening dress, albeit one that's pinching a little too tight. This girl is actually wearing a jumper and it's got a roll neck collar which goes right up her neck to her chin. She looks the most out-of-place person in the room as the men are smart, but casual, nothing but dinner jackets. And there's plenty of food being consumed.

Because of the third car, I wonder if this is a mother and daughter or maybe they've got a friend over. The conversation is pretty inane, talk of jobs and of the weather, then a little bit about golf. There's nothing, no nugget of juice and I'm finding it all a little bit banal. I ease around to the back door and find it unlocked. Inside is a little kitchen which I will need to get through it to get to the hall. I close the door quietly behind me and feel the prickles on my skin. It doesn't matter how many times you do it, when you're crawling around with other people there, it affects you. You start to sweat a little because the house is stifling.

I hear the noise at the dinner table and there's a push back of a chair, so quickly I step across the kitchen, sliding into the dark hallway, never looking back, but getting to the stairs and stepping up them quietly. When I'm at the top of the stairs, I stop and listen. There are dishes being cleared away in the kitchen, so maybe the guests will be leaving soon. Maybe they'll move through somewhere else.

It takes about five minutes before they retire to another room which is on the ground floor and I can still hear them. I head into the bedrooms. The first one's a large double with an en suite. It's probably the master bedroom of the house. There are silk sheets, and everything just looks like it has that little bit of a feminine touch. Proper class. I open the wardrobe finding the male side first. There's a lot of jackets, some Tweed, quite stylish, plenty of shirts, all neatly ironed, tie rack, consummate businessmen; there's golf slacks as well. Some Pringle jumpers.

It's all fairly standard fare for a man of his age.

Then I skip across to the other wardrobe, which is full of women's clothes. Light dress jackets, some trousers, some skirts, a few dresses. Again, nothing unusual. There's a third section to the wardrobe and when I pull it back, I nearly collapse on the floor. I wasn't expecting the array of nightwear that's in there. I think they call it playwear, although I'm not familiar with it myself. Let's just say it's designed to enhance certain features. That's probably the best way to talk about it. Because when I imagine these people wearing it, it's not an image I want. These are not people from beauty magazines or any of those other magazines people might read, but hey ho, if it floats your boat and it keeps the marriage together who cares. It's not a crime. And I start to think that maybe they're struggling and maybe their marriage is in trouble and this is what they're doing. Maybe it's gone too far, and that's why he's seeing Alison Hadleigh. I don't put any conclusion on this. It's just the thoughts running through my head.

I stop and listen, hearing them downstairs again. For a brief moment, somebody opens the door and climbs the stairs. I get down behind the bed, but I needn't have feared. They're doing what most people do in these circumstances, up to visit the toilet. A couple of minutes, then back down the stairs. I continue to the next bedroom which looks like a guest bedroom because it's fairly banal. Nicely decorated, but there's no personal touch. There're no photographs.

The third bedroom upstairs is fairly similar. I see no presence of a younger person's items. Maybe she's not the daughter. I did a quick sweep of the bathroom and find only two toothbrushes so there's nothing indicating a third person in the house. Sneaking back down, I creep along the hallway when I hear someone get up in the lounge. Like a lot of houses, there's a cupboard under the stairs. I pull it, see a horde of cleaning equipment, step inside and pull it shut. Sitting in the darkness, I start to think what I'd tell people if they open the door. I have a beanie hat that I can pull down and become a balaclava. I ideally don't want to frighten people like this, running off as the one-armed burglar. Part of me wishes I had brought the prosthetic along with me, but it just gets in the way. So, if I have to, I'll run off and hope they don't spot the fact there's only one arm. Maybe throw a punch or two.

There you go, there was no need to fear. They're going upstairs. And I think, upstairs? When I hear the lights go out, a click of the switch, after four people have climbed the stairs, I step out. I give it a minute lest people are running about the landing above, but once I'm satisfied people have made it to bedrooms, I sneak quickly back up the stairs, listening in on the voices I heard before. The older woman is in the main bedroom, but it's not John Carson I hear in with her. It's the other voice. There's a clear distinction, as the man has a strong Glasgow brogue. The other room's quieter. And I hear John Carson and the occasional word from the younger girl. There's a lot of what I would call schmoozing, compliments, and then I descend the stairs. It's all getting a bit personal. I'm not one to sit and listen at the doors when people are getting their rocks off. I've had to do it routinely—bad wives and husbands before—and it's a very depressing part of the job. And besides, this is telling me nothing.

So, I head downstairs and start searching around the living room and the dining area. The living room looks like any other normal family. There's only the two of them and there's lots of photographs, especially of the golf club tournaments. I see the judge in a few of them, and there's even a picture of Alison Hadleigh with Russell. And then I see John Carson with the large woman. That must be his wife, but yet he's upstairs in a room with the young girl and nobody seems to be complaining. The penny is beginning to drop on me. And I think I might know his relationship with Alison Hadleigh. Her profile is taking an unexpected twist. But I'm thorough if nothing else, so I'll search the rest of the house.

I step outside and walk over to the garage. It's locked with one of those roll up doors. I'll make an absolute racket if I open it. So, I drift back inside the house looking for that little group of keys everybody keeps somewhere. Sure enough, there's a key rack just beside the cooker. I take a selection, step outside and have the garage door open in no time. I make my way back, hang up the keys, except for the garage one. Stepping inside I don't switch on the light, but I can still see about halfway along the garage where it's been halved off with an interior wall. It looks like it's been built as an afterthought. The front half contains a lot of tools, lawn mower, everything you'd expect in a garage.

I step forward carefully in the dark, moving around objects until I reach that door in the centre of the interstitial wall. Pushing the door open, I step inside, and something nearly strikes me from the side. It's totally dark on this side, so I get my mobile and flick on the light from it, quickly checking there's no windows. Running the light across a wall, I first of all reel in shock, but inside part of me is laughing. You're usually on edge when doing these things, but at the moment I'm doing everything I can not to clasp my hand around my mouth and just let rip with the belly laugh.

There's an assorted array of whips across the back wall.

There's a machine on the left-hand side that, well, I wouldn't say I don't know what it's for, but I haven't seen any of these in operation and it's not something I want to use myself. There are handcuffs and lots of other equipment for restraining. However, it's not restraining in the sense of violence, a lot of its play-like. There's soft padding around it, or else it's furriness. Some of it's got pink around the edge of the cuffs. You've either been arrested by the fairy police or this is a little dungeon for someone. I've never been in one of these but like most people, you hear the talk and you've maybe seen one of those ridiculous programs on the TV detailing people's lives.

People enjoy this sort of thing. But my impression of John Carson has changed. I sweep the garage thoroughly though just in case there's anything else. But I find nothing. As I'm exiting the garage the lights are back on in the house, which makes my getaway a little bit more awkward. So, I hang fire behind one of the cars and see the two couples exiting the front door. There are hugs all around and kisses on the cheek. But I notice John Carson with his hand on the younger woman. He's got her shoulder and there's a sense of gratitude from him. I'm a bit confused, but then I don't know how you sign off after that sort of a night. It's all very genteel hugs and kisses before the Glasgow man and the young woman drive off. I'll make a note of their registration, but I'm not going to tail them. It might all look a bit kinky, but it's all pretty innocent too.

As John and his wife are waving goodbye to the couple, I sneak back into the kitchen, put the key back on the rack, come back through the rear door to my hidey-hole behind the car. Seeing the house is in darkness and they've disappeared upstairs again, I make my way quickly and quietly back to my own car. And sitting down, I realize my hand doesn't have that little shake. When you're investigating, and especially when you're up close like this, sneaking around the place, the adrenaline pours through, but not today. Today there's a laugh deep down in my belly but I sit there professionally, holding it in.

Turning the key, I drive until I see a sign of a burger joint. I pull inside, get an order of coffee and one of those burgers that doesn't really do a lot for you, sit down, and start to eat. And then I just laugh. I can't help it. I just laugh. Not even that weird look of the girl behind the counter bothers me. A dungeon. A dungeon in your garage.

Chapter 14

I roll into Alison Hadleigh's house at seven in the morning. She's up and prancing about in the kitchen, making her breakfast. She asks if I'll sit down with her and just update her on where I'm at. If I want, I can have an omelette. I'm tired, but she's the client and she does deserve an update, even if I'm not ready to give one properly. So, over an omelette, coffee, and a good deal of sultry looks, I tell her I think I may know where her husband is, but I'm not quite sure what's happened to him.

It's still a fabrication, but it leaves me open if he's still alive at the end of it. I tell her it should only be a couple of days and then hopefully I can have the whole thing straightened out. She looks at me quizzically as I recount these things, but then just seems to nod. It's at the end of the meal I get a rather unusual offer.

'Paddy,' she says, 'obviously you've been out all night, but I was wondering if you'd like to keep me company this morning. I was just going to top up my tan at the back. I could do with a little help. I usually sit in my conservatory, let the sunshine through there. It's a little more discreet. You don't have to wear as much as if you would at the back in the garden.'

'Actually, I'm exhausted,' I say, 'and you're right. I've been out all night, so I'm going to bed this morning.'

She looks somewhat disappointed, but then says, 'But if you're up this afternoon, I can still be here.' She's quite insatiable. And even now she parades around in her dressing gown. I get the feeling a lot of it is trying to entice me but given the company that she keeps, it's starting to form some ideas in my head. One of which is making me think, *Is the judge involved in this? Was he part of this lifestyle of hers? Has she been to the dungeon?* She's quite a forceful character. A part of my mind suddenly thinks what character she plays in that dungeon. Maybe she's not the 'handcuffed woman', desperately crying out for a master. Maybe she's on the other side. Maybe it's a dominant woman these men like. And that's where I stop because it's all getting a little bit beyond what I'm comfortable with. I chuckle, what I think is inwardly, but obviously not.

'What's the matter, Paddy? What's so funny?'

'Just something I saw reminded me of you. It's nothing. Don't think twice about it. I'm off to bed.' I sleep through until three o'clock. After getting up, I make my way to the shower and enjoy the warm water coursing over my body. I'm tired. I'm not in my own bed, and that always bothers me since I've been sailing on Craigantlet for such a long time. The waves are quite soothing at night, giving a totally different feel, and something you miss. I also know I'm going to be up tonight, as I'm planning to go out to where the judge is hiding. I'll break in and see if I can find anything else. I need to understand the relationship between Russell Hadleigh and Laura Sutherland. Are they business partners? Was he partly linked into this Russian connection, as well? And if so, and they want rid of him, why is she protecting him? What's going on? As I stand there in the shower it suddenly occurs to me that maybe I'm not being open enough with my employer. Maybe she can garner some information.

With this in mind, I step out of the bathroom, towel wrapped around my waist, only to be confronted by her as I opened the door. She's stood in her bikini, and the lack of it was quite a shock. It's a deliberate attempt to lure me back to her idea of sunbathing in her conservatory but frankly, it's a little forward and rather unappealing, like somebody throwing all their cash in front of you telling you how rich they are. Don't get me wrong, she's got looks for her age. She's incredibly good looking, but I don't like this. It's like there's a carrot being held in front of my face and I'm meant to follow, and I don't work like that. But I do need information.

'Ah, you're up and about, Paddy,' she says, and I feel her scan my body. 'I'm still downstairs in the conservatory if you want to come down. Do you think the tan's working?'

'It seems to be doing all right,' I say. 'But I'm grand.'

'Are you sure?' she says. 'You look to me like a mammoth that's weary. You could do with a bit of a back rub, let someone manipulate those muscles with their hands. I've been told I'm particularly good at it.'

'I'm fine,' I say. 'Well, what's all this in need of? Are you just someone who likes the sun?'

She laughs. 'We live on the outskirts of Stranraer. If I liked the sun, I'd be in Ibiza. I've got an important date on Saturday evening and I need to get ready for it. I've got to look my best.'

I nod and turn away, but a thought snaps me back. 'Really?' I say, 'How much are you showing? When people look their best, they usually throw a bit of makeup on. But you seem to want to bronze your whole body.'

'I wonder if you could be invited along,' she says. 'It's a rather fun event. We engage in one of those little roleplay things.'

I feign innocence. 'Roleplay? Are you one of those Dungeons and Dragons people? Some sort of fantasy?'

'Yes, Paddy. That's what it is, fantasy. I have to dress up as an Amazon, so I need to have my skin looking its best.'

I nod and turn away into my room, but then turn back again. 'Oh,' I say, 'I just heard something about the golf club, and I wonder if you could help me with it.'

'Yes?' she says, inching her way forward into my room. I'm not comfortable because she slides past me and sits herself down on my bed. But I need the information.

'I was talking to some of them up at the club, and they said Russell quite often played with a female golfer.'

'Oh, yes. He played a couple of times with that young girl, Susan something,' she said. 'Really good, Russell said. Beat the pants off him. Quite young, too. I did get a bit worried about him. But he said he was old enough to be her granddad. He quite liked her. But I think that was all it was. Just an old man staring at his youth.'

'Yes, I've met her,' I say. 'and the pro says she's good. But it wasn't her I was thinking of. Someone named Laura.'

At this point, I see the steam coming out of the ears, the body tenses. She's no longer taking that relaxed, laidback approach to me. Instead, something's charging through her head, somewhere angry and she's no longer trying to entice me. She's suddenly enraged but not with me, it's with the memory of something.

'Yes,' she says in a controlled voice. 'I do remember him mentioning her. Not much of a looker, if I remember right.'

'Oh, you've met her?' I said.

'I saw her once if you remember the photograph you showed me that Russell insists on remaining on our wall. Cheap little tart. I doubt I'd give her the time of the day. Very forward with men. Always flaunting, Paddy. You know the kind of woman I'm talking about.'

I find the statement rather ironic, but I nod my head in assent, anyway. I've clearly hit a nerve. So instead of backing away, I trudge on in.

'So, did your husband play a round with her?'

She stands up instantly off the bed and steps towards me. 'You know I caught them, but that little trollop would tie in with anyone. That little trollop would take over any man for her own needs.' With that she starts to exit the room.

'Sorry,' I say, 'I didn't mean to upset. I meant a round of golf.'

She stops, turns around with a smile. 'Ah, sorry. I thought you meant something else,' she says. 'Of course, you wouldn't be so indiscreet.'

I can see she's still trembling, anger seething underneath but she's forcing herself to remain calm and the poise is back. The one that says, 'Come and catch me.' The one that says, 'This is available, and you will not resist.' In some ways I find it quite desperate and as I said before, that's no turn on. But for the sake of the relationship we have, I decide I'd better offer her a little bit of rope.

'I'd love to, but I've got to go out. Another time, but if you've got a back rub, I can't do anything for this knot between my shoulders. I'd love to have you deal with it.'

She steps back into the room, slides herself around me, and places her hands between my shoulders. Soon she's working away at them and to my surprise, she's particularly good. I was going to make my excuses, but I'll give her two or three minutes because, actually, I'm quite sore back there. She stands awfully close and I can smell the perfume. I reckon it's recent because it's very intense, like it's just been put on. Was she seriously waiting for me to get up? Has she been hunting me all day? Alison Hadleigh obviously has needs, and whether or not Russell wasn't satisfying them or they're just excessive needs, I don't know. But what I do know is I won't be counted amongst her number.

'I really need to get going and I'm probably going to be out tonight,' I say. 'But I should be back in the morning. Maybe I'll update you at coffee again.'

'That'd be good,' she says. 'But if you come in and I'm not up, just come up to the bedroom and give me a knock on the door. If you don't hear anything step on in and wake me up properly.' There's a flash in her eyes. And I know what that statement means, but I'm fairly sure I could raise the hounds of hell knocking on her door, so it won't come to that.

I have dinner out, picking up Susan after she finishes her work at the golf club and taking her to a local cafe. She's full of chat, excited to be working with me . . . and wanting to know when we can meet next. I tell her I need her up at the golf club keeping an eye on things. Specifically, if Sergei is there at any point, and if Laura plays a round again. I also ask her about Laura and the judge—did she ever see anything between them? She says that her sister who had started working at the club, when Susan was a lot younger, came back once and told her about this strange four-ball that went out.

It was John Carson, the judge, Laura, and the judge's wife. Apparently, there'd been blows on the way round and when they were in the bar afterwards, it all came to a head. There was shouting and screaming. The judge's wife had walked out, quickly followed by John Carson. She said what struck her was the fact that her sister had been talking about handcuffs. The row had been over handcuffs.

By now, I'm getting a very sordid idea of what goes on behind closed doors in this community. I think there may be two things going on at once, but who knows exactly what about each thing, I don't know. There's some sort of play ring going on. How many have seen John Carson's dungeon? And is there something going on with the shop with the Russian connection? Have things gone sour there that's causing a further rift, and is there anything left over from those days of roleplay?

I take Susan home and spend the evening in a small cafe looking through some more communications from Martha. She says she's employed another contact of ours and believes that she may be able to intercept some communications coming from the Russians. I tell her not to put the person at risk, as I think these guys are serious. To do it from a distance, highly covert, make sure there's no risk of getting caught. She agrees, but says she'll update me as and when.

I sit and ponder what I'm going to do. One of the things I can do is hand everything over to the police. But really, I need to check with my client and what she wants because if her husband's implicated, I might not get my fee. At the end of the day, we all have to make our bread and butter. But on the other hand, do I simply keep going? I get the feeling that Alison might like revenge on Laura, but at the moment she wants to keep Russell, as well. At least that's what I'm guessing.

It's about eleven o'clock when I finally wind out of that cafe, having drunk about four cups of coffee. I'm usually a tea man, but I'm feeling a little jaded and need pepped up tonight. Getting into my car, I drive out towards Russell's hideout, parking up some distance from it. I'm putting on my black gear because I'm breaking in and put my prosthetic on, as well. Always handy in case you're seen, even if it does make the act of moving around stealthily a little bit more awkward.

The car's parked about half a mile away and I'll be running through the fields along the coast road until I get up to the house the judge is staying in. I sit and watch it for twenty minutes, making sure no one else is around. Just then, I see a figure strolling casually along the road. It might look like a normal man out for a walk except he's six foot four and he's got shoulders that we'd need to widen doors for. He also is watching the house incredibly well. He's scanning into the undergrowth around it, and I make sure I'm hidden well down. But what he's not doing is covering up his intention to scan the house, which makes me think that the person inside knows he's there.

There's a light on and I reckon the judge is still up. So once the man's gone past, I sneak across to the side of the building, keeping myself tight against the wall. I can hear classical music playing and it's hard to hear the judge's movements. Taking a little mirror on a stick, I prop it up to the bottom of the window and look in to see him enjoying a brandy in a chair, listening away to his music. Retracting my device, I step around the building to the front door. There's no one out on the street beneath us, so I try to open the door, but there's a physical bar there this time.

I race back to the rear of the house, just in case the man is strolling around again. I find a window. It's one of those old shutter types and doesn't take long to throw it up. I climb inside one of the unlit rooms. With the shutter down behind me, I find a dark corner and listen, trying to work out if anything else is happening in the house. There's nothing. And so I start to creep around the kitchen I've landed in.

There's simply plain food, basic rations. Everything to keep yourself going. I don't know, was I expecting bits of paper? If there was, what would he do with him? Would he hide them? What sort of paper am I looking for? As I'm just about finished with searching the kitchen, I hear movement. Bending in behind where the door would swing open, I stay quiet and low as I hear feet in the hallway outside. They turn off elsewhere.

Once everything is quiet again, I carefully open the kitchen door and see a dark hall leading through to an unlit room at the end. There's a bedroom in the middle. I begin to hear the faint snores of the judge and I sneak along quietly into the far room to begin a search of it. There's a television' and a small radio on a fireplace that hasn't been lit. There are radiators supplied from the oil tank outside, and everything seems pretty normal. On a shelf on the side, I find a newspaper. Also, several little bits and bobs that have always been shoved through the letter box, sale for this, buy computers from here, that sort of thing.

With nothing found, I walk along to the bedroom. I hear a man inside roaring in his sleep so carefully open the door and look inside. And he's there, sprawled out on top of the bed in his underpants. It's not a glamorous sight, and I'm not particularly keen to search the room. It's just that if I don't, I won't know if he's got something on his person. There's a single wardrobe and a dresser so I move to the dresser first, finding empty drawers. It's not unusual and I guess he's not here for long. I turn to the wardrobe, opening it quietly. I'm not worried if he wakes up because I have my balaclava on, he won't know who I am. I'll look like a simple thief. But I am keen to go through the pockets in his jackets. There are two jackets inside the wardrobe, and a couple of pairs of trousers. On the floor of the wardrobe is a small suitcase. I bend down and search it but find it's been emptied completely.

Going to the jackets, I reach inside and find one small piece of paper. It's a betting slip that's showing a two-hundred-grand bet. Well, I guess you'd have to get a receipt for that sort of money. It's the three o'clock in Ayr, two weeks ago. I place it on the floor, take out a small camera with a flash, and shut the wardrobe door around it. I take the picture quickly before returning the slip back inside the jacket pocket. A further search of the clothing reveals nothing further.

I think I'm done inside the house, so I quickly make my way to the back window again. I step out, closing it down. Sneak around to the side of the house, I look out to the road for my man. There's no one there. Looking up and down, I can't see anyone. It's then I feel a hand on my shoulder. I'm spun around. And the first thing I see is a large fist planting itself on the side of my face.

Chapter 15

I manage to get my arm up to block the second punch at my head but the first is still ringing. The man then reaches forward, grabs my shoulders and drives a knee up into my gut. He's got six inches on me and he brings it all into play as he lifts me up and throws me to one side. I crack my head off the wall and fall to the ground. I haven't got time to check whether or not I'm bleeding before he's over me again. He's pinned me up now against the wall, his hand around my throat and my one good arm is grabbing it. Maybe he's finding it a bit bizarre that my other hand just simply sits there. Maybe he's not bothered, but he continues to squeeze on my throat.

'What are you doing in there?' he says in a menacing voice.

'Nothing,' I say, 'nothing. Look, I've taken nothing.' I try to play the role of the burglar hoping he buys this. Even if he phones the police, what's the worst they're going to do? Charge me with breaking and entering. And if they go to do that, I'll simply spill the beans on what's going on. I've got a few friends in constabulary and they can sort this out. What bothers me more is if he thinks he doesn't want any witnesses around here.

'Look, I've got nothing. I did try, I went in, but there's nothing to take. I've stolen nothing.'

'You little rat,' says the man. 'You don't know what's good for you. I don't want to see you here again. Do you understand me?' I nod furiously and he delivers a punch to my stomach that nearly makes me puke. 'Get your stupid ass out of here,' he says. He turns me, then kicks my backside which makes me sprawl to the floor. 'And do it quietly.' He follows up with a second kick to my ass just as I'm able to stand back up again. I don't hang about, leaving the building and heading into some foliage as soon as I can. Somewhere to just stop, kneel down, and let my head recover.

He nailed me really well in the guts. I'm breathing hard, but I don't want to hop straight to my car in case I'm being tailed and give away what that looks like. He didn't remove my balaclava which tells me that my story of being a basic thief must have worked. He's trying to scare me off. Maybe that's what he's here for, basic protection. He certainly didn't have a Russian voice. So, someone else might have put him here.

I wonder if the judge will move now. It was always a possibility. After twenty minutes, I see no one else around and the man is back doing his patrol in front of the house. With that I head to the car, drive off a little way and just rest up. Feeling the back of my head I think I've had a cut. Placing my hand up and bringing it back I can see the blood. My hair's matted at the back and as I take the mask off, in the car light in the little mirror, I can see there's a cracking bruise developing on my cheek. I'll tell you something, if I see that man again, and he doesn't see me coming, I'm going to crack him one back. But that's not good practice, best just to leave it as a sloppy. He shouldn't have caught me. Maybe I'm tired. Or maybe I was preoccupied with that betting slip I found.

I sit in the dark on my mobile, tracing back the results

of previous weeks from Ayr racecourse. The horse's name, Mighty Drive. Well it would have to be wouldn't it, but it's not listed in the top three. When I do find it, it appears it came in lame, last, having pulled up halfway round. Whether that means there was any shenanigans I don't know. But what I do know is that bet was no good and that was two-hundred grand. I'm sure the judge has money, but I don't think he's got two-hundred grand to throw away. Why would he think it was such a sure bet? So where did the two-hundred grand come from and has it got something to do with why the Russians are after him? And does it have something to do with why Angus Porterfield was chopped up into pieces and left in the shed at the back of the twelfth?

I put this all down in writing and send it off to Martha to see if she can dig anything up on the net. But I doubt it. I tell her that having made the money, it seems strange to be withdrawn. So, if she can get into his bank account and find out if anything's gone from there, that would be great, but I'm not expecting it. I'm expecting this came in a suitcase, possibly to Angus Porterfield, and then Russell's taken it. He's seen a bet, but why such a sure bet? Maybe that's one to run past Susan, is there anyone at the club involved with their racecourse or with horses?

I spin past the house in the car and I spot the man walking up and down in front. He still looks enormous, but I guess the judge is still there. If he thought he'd been compromised properly, I guess he would have been gone. It's on the second pass an hour later that I see the judge at the front of the house in the morning sunlight having a quick stretch while the large man's walking along the road and glancing over at him. But neither shows signs of any interest in the other. This makes me wonder, is he employed by the judge or is someone else protecting the judge? Too many questions and my head is really groggy.

I had said that I'd brief Alison Hadleigh in the morning, but to be quite frank, I feel like rubbish. I could do with an undisturbed shower and someone to take a look at the back of my head. Alison Hadleigh will no doubt try and get me into bed and I'm really not up for that at this time. She's too crass with it. It's about eight o'clock and I know Susan will have started work at the golf club, so I choose to go that way instead. I do a quick change at the roadside, putting on a pair of slacks and a polo shirt.

When I turn up at the golf club, minus my prosthetic arm, I find her again in the shop. She's about to go out for a round on her own. 'I'll quit practice,' she says, 'cause you look like you need the help.' She takes me through to an outbuilding, a kind of storeroom, where they put the bottles, and there she looks at my head. She's not delicate, and I'm not sure if she's done this before, but she says it's definitely cut although the bleeding's stopped. And it's a mass of clumped hair.

'Do you think it needs to be looked at?' I ask. 'Like in a hospital?'

'I really don't know,' she says. 'I could get my sister to look at it. She's had first aid training. In fact, something a little bit more than that. So, she'd probably be able to patch it up for you, and if it really needs something, I could even get mom to look at it.'

'That might be the best solution,' I say, 'if she'd be up for it. Is she at home?'

'She's just come off night shift. She's a nurse up at the hospital, but I'm sure she'd look at it for you. I'll give her a call.'

Half an hour later I'm sat in the kitchen of Susan's house. Her mother's dressed in jeans and a tee shirt and is working at the back of my head as she felt it needed a couple of stitches. When I said I didn't want to go to the hospital she simply accepted it and started patching me up herself. She said it wouldn't be perfect and that she'd take a look at it again in a couple of days if I wanted her to. I thank her, but she tells Susan to pop out by the garage to get some bacon for her to cook. Susan says she thinks that there's bacon in the house, but her mom insists. As soon as she's out the door, the woman sits down in front of me.

'Thank you kindly,' I say, 'it's much appreciated.'

'It's the least I could do, Mr Smythe considering the fact you're all that Susan's been talking about these last few days. Just who are you and what are you wanting with my daughter?'

I look at the woman and she seems like an honest mom just watching out for her daughter. She's got Susan's looks as well. Obviously older but when she was eighteen, I'm sure she was a figure chased by all the boys. Even now with my older eye, she certainly looks like a fine woman; her straightforwardness and honesty are also quite engaging.

'Okay,' I say, 'the honest truth is I've been engaged in my capacity as a private eye to investigate some local people. One of the places they frequented was the golf club, and your daughter has been invaluable in providing me information about them. At the start she was quite infatuated with me, but I've made it clear that that's something that's not going to happen. If anything, I've tried to act like a big brother. I'm hoping she's understanding that.'

'Well, I agree with you,' says the woman, 'and you can call me

Maggie, Maggie Calderwood, because I noticed you haven't asked.'

'Well, no, I didn't know how much you wanted me to know about you. It makes people uncomfortable sometimes in case they think I'll run a background check on them or something.'

'Would you?'

'Yes, I would if I thought there was an issue, but Susan has been extremely helpful, as has Kirsten, your other daughter. Although, I think Kirsten's a lot more wary of me, which is a good trait.'

The woman steps away and puts the kettle on. We remain in silence for a couple of minutes until she gives me a steaming cup of black coffee. She gulps down about half of hers and looks me in the eye. 'She says that you're happy to take her on, as help. Don't string her along. If it's a proper job tell me about it and tell me if it's safe. I don't mind her running errands for you and things like that, but if it's going to be dangerous, she is only a teen, and she does need trained.'

'I'll try my best not to put her at any risk,' I say, 'but in my line of work things sometimes blindside you. And she's also very keen to get involved, but very naive. I'll keep her out of it. Certainly, I'll keep her out of anything dangerous. She tailed me once to somewhere that really, I didn't want her to be, but I managed the situation and she was kept safe. And since then, I've tried to maintain that distance.'

'Yeah, but she wants in. Susan's talked about the police before, but I think she sees your line of work as more exciting. You ever been a policeman, Mr Smythe?'

'Yes, I was,' I say, 'back home in Ulster. But then I lost the arm and it was going to be desk work with me after that. So, I went out on my own and it's worked out for me.'

The woman steps forward. She puts her hand on my cheek. 'That's quite a bruise you got there. How'd you get it?'

'I was out tailing a suspect, had to break in and search their place. When I got out, I got caught by someone. Luckily, they thought I was a burglar and they didn't want me about. That's the truth, Maggie. If these sorts of things are not what you want for your daughter, then I'll push her away, absolutely.'

The woman walks to the window and looks out of it. Then she turns back to me. 'Susan may not have told you, but her father was lost in the line of protecting people. He was a soldier, protecting refugees far away and ever since she was that little girl, she's wanted to be that type of person. So, I won't stop her going down that route. But I want to know about you, Mr Smythe, are you on that side or are you just someone taking the money?'

'I won't lie to you,' I say. 'That's the type of person I aim to be, but the waters get muddy. There is no black and white quite often. And yes, often I hand things to the police. Often, I hand things back to clients to make the decision of what they want to do. But I'll let her have her own integrity. If she's not comfortable with something, I won't push her to do it.' The woman steps forward, crouches down in front of me looking up into my eyes and just stares. It's deeply disconcerting and I look away.

'Don't do that, please—just look at me,' she says, and I do. It's almost like she's sensing something. Or is she chewing over the facts of what I said? Then she puts her hand forward and I shake it. 'You can call me Maggie anytime. And if you need me, I'm here. But understand,' she says, 'if Susan gets hurt in the line of work, that's fine, but if she gets hurts emotionally or you become anything else other than an employer or anything more than a big brother, then I will come for you.'

I look at the woman and laugh. 'I like you, Maggie. I see where she gets her spirit from.' As the woman stands up and turns away, Susan comes in the door. I pick up my coffee and drink. *She certainly comes from good stock, Susan,* I think. *Determined. That's a woman that's brought up kids on her own. Knows the lay of the land, but also is willing to trust. Yeah, she comes from good stock.*

As I'm sitting there, I get a message from Martha. She's got information that the delivery's arriving in Scotland on Sunday. That's tomorrow when I've already got the stakeout tonight for Alison's big party at the hotel. I'm thinking what's best and reckon that Susan could come to the hotel with me and do that stakeout. She'd be useful as well because there may be people she knows and I don't, but the Russian gig is not happening for her. Maggie serves up bacon and eggs and Susan sits opposite me, smiling, awaiting whatever words I'm going to say. Maggie sits chugging more coffee.

'Susan,' I say, 'I think you might be up for a little stakeout tonight.' She looks at me, quizzically. "There's a meeting in a hotel. It's not the Russians. It's my employer. And I want to see what she's up to. I'm not quite sure how we'll do it or what we'll have to do but someone of your age could easily pass for a maid or a cleaner, much easier than a one-armed man. Are you up for that tonight?'

Her face is abeam, and she looks at her mom, as if she wants permission. But Maggie shakes her head and I see Susan's face fall.

'It's not up to me, Susan. I told Mr Smythe I'm happy for him to take you on board. You're eighteen, it's your decision, and he knows where I stand with everything.'

Susan's face becomes wide with a beaming smile again. 'Great, Paddy. When do we go?' she says.

'Scheduled for eight tonight. And you might know the hotel; I did give you a request to check up on it.' Her face suddenly becomes even more excited and she disappears from the room before bringing back some A4 sheets. I scan them quickly and they show the Riverside Hotel, one proprietor, Matthew Laurel. It's small, twenty rooms and looks ideal for the sort of thing Alison's group might want.

'Good stuff,' I say, 'useful, all extremely useful. Make sure you're au fait with this by tonight. I'll pick you up about seven. Also, an all-black set of clothing, some normal clothing and possibly something dressy. And a maid's outfit. Nothing outlandish, just a normal cleaning coat. If we need something different, we need something different.

She smiles and I announce I need to go. Maggie gets up and says she'll see me to the door. In fact, she walks me all the way out to my car where she gets me to roll down the window once I've got inside.

'Take care of her tonight, Paddy,' she says. And then she stops just looking at me and I look back. 'If you ever want a drink,' she says, 'and I mean a drink, give me a bell.' She produces a piece of paper and writes her number on it. 'It's not easy being a single mom, and even though they're older, I don't get out that much. Most of the men you meet, they just want something else and I've lost contact with most of my girlfriends. These two took a lot of looking after. So, if you ever want a chat, or just go to the cinema or something,' she says, 'I don't mind. You look a bit of a lonely guy yourself.'

I take the piece of paper from our hand, look at the number and then smile. 'Sure,' I say, 'sure.' She gives a nervous smile back then walks to the front door of the house where she turns and watches me as I start the car. She gives a little wave. I probably pause too long looking back. It's an idea, I think, but not for now. I know some company would be good when this is all done.

Chapter 16

I place a call to Alison Hadleigh and when she answers, the tone in her voice tells me she's not that happy. 'You said you were going to update me at breakfast,' she says, 'and now, here it is, how much later in the day, and you still haven't got to me.'

'Sorry,' I say. 'Last night got a little bit unexpectedly rough, but I'm definitely getting closer. I should have something for you soon.'

'Why haven't you got something for me now?' asks Alison.

'As I said, last night got a little bit rough. I don't want information in your hands that could be dangerous to you until I'm sure that I've got other ends tied up.' This sounds like a rather noble gesture and hopefully she's buying it because, frankly, it's a load of rubbish. I still am not sure where her husband stands, or where she stands. Until I do, I'm not getting caught in the crossfire.

'While I've got you, Paddy,' she says, and the voice has changed to a softer lilt, 'are you out and about this evening? Because if you're not, I'd like you to come out with me. I've got a few friends who would like to meet you.'

'I hope you haven't been telling the world about who I am and what I do,' I say to her, sounding shocked, but inside reckoning

I know what's coming.

'No, no,' she says. 'I've just been telling a few friends about this strange man I've met. I think you could have a good evening off with me. We only ever seem to meet round the breakfast table when you're busy with work. I'd quite like to see what you're like when you're not working.'

'You're my employer. You're paying me. That's why I always seem like I'm working.'

'Really?' she says. 'It hardly seems like I see you at all, you're so busy. Come with me tonight; I'm meeting some friends at a hotel.' I reckon I can get some information, so I decide to play along.

'It sounds interesting. And to do what? Have a meal, some drinks?'

'Yes,' says Alison, 'for starters. Then we'll see what fun the evening brings.'

'What's the hotel?' I say.

'The Riverside,' she says, and starts giving me directions towards it. I listen, taking it in, but I already know where it is. 'It's a good group of people,' she says, 'and sometimes you never quite know where the night leads.' Every time she finishes a sentence, it has that hanging unknown, but it sounds risqué, not risky.

'And what time would you be looking for me to be there?'

'Well, you can meet me here at half seven. We'd get there for eight. You don't have to dress up too smart. In honesty, the clothes you wear don't matter that much at this. I'm sure we can find you something suitable if you haven't got anything.'

'Half seven it is then,' I say, and her voice suddenly goes quiet.

'So, you haven't got anything on my husband? Do you still think he's dead or is he missing?'

'As I said, I do have some things, and it's looking like he may still be alive, but I can't guarantee it. I need to do a little bit more digging, but I'll let you know as soon as I have something concrete.'

'Please do,' she says, and she sounds relieved. I'm struggling to get behind the mentality of someone who's one minute asking me off to some rather strange evening do, with a sultry voice, and who then seems to be panicking about whether or not her husband is alive. But, you know, I've seen stranger in my time. People are people and there's no working them out sometimes.

I end the call and disappear off to the seaside for a while. I just need a bit of a rest if I'm going to be out all night tonight. About an hour and a half later, I call Alison Hadleigh up again, making my excuses for that evening, as it seems that there's a major line of inquiry I need to follow. It's regarding her husband. I make it sound quite earnest, and she buys it. There seems to be a sadness in her voice, but also a joy when I mention her husband. It's getting quite scary, the fact that she was really looking forward to this evening, and I wonder what plans she had for me, given the room at the back of John Carson's garage. But tonight's plans are already made.

So, after kipping in my car, I pop round later that afternoon to pick up Susan at seven. She's dressed appropriately, mainly in black, her red hair tied up at the back. She's as keen as mustard, smiling at me, but not like she did at the start. It's now just genuine excitement for the job, and I realize part of the allure that she had for me was what I did, not who I am. It's not that big a surprise to an older man and it makes me glad that I didn't make any moves. Not only would it have been ridiculously wrong, given her age, but also it would have been very hollow. The girl's in love with the intrigue, not with the investigator. But my ego was built up again as Maggie comes to the door to wave her off.

We don't exchange words but there's a broad smile for me. I take a moment to smile and reciprocate back. When it's all over and done, I might take her up on the offer of a coffee or a cinema visit. I could do with some downtime.

As we drive out of Stranraer, the town's coming alive for Saturday night, but we're heading slightly further out until we see the small hotel and its grounds, believe it or not, by a river. The Riverside Inn is somewhat dilapidated, but there's already a number of cars sitting outside. I believe they have the full run of the hotel.

With it being late, I decide to park a little distance away and I walk Susan through some fields and hedgerows until we can get a good view of the entrance. I hand her a pair of binoculars and tell her to watch the front door, advising me if she sees Alison Hadleigh, or anyone else we know. As a quarter to eight approaches, she says, 'There's Alison Hadleigh arriving alone.' I grab the binoculars and sure enough, she's looking well made up, hair obviously been done recently, a red dress cut extremely low, and with high heels that could give you vertigo. She looks like the fox on the prowl, and I'm feeling even more glad that I'm here as an onlooker and not a participant.

I hand the binoculars back to Susan and take a run around the building. Minding the hedges and trees, I look at all the exits and entrances. When I come back, Susan's got a look of delight on her face.

'Do you want a list?' she says.

'A list of what?'

'Of the guests. It's like a who's who from the golf club. I've seen twenty people go in,' she says, 'and I can name fifteen of them.'

'Really?' I say. 'What sort of age groups are they?'

'Mainly your sort of age, that older bracket.' This makes me feel fantastic, as you can imagine, but I ignore the slur and ask if there's any others. 'Yes,' she says. 'A couple of younger men, one or two younger women, but not many. The majority is older.'

'Couples?' I say.

'Again, mainly,' she says. 'One or two are people I know who aren't married but have brought somebody with them. That's usually where the younger people have come in. There's no younger couple.'

'So, an escort. Do you think they'd be paid escorts?'

Susan was looking at me in shock, and I have to remind myself she hasn't yet made her twenties. Maybe the ways of the world haven't hit home fully. Not in the personal sense, just in the fact of how extreme people can get looking for company.

'So, when do we go inside?' says Susan. 'Do you need me to get changed?'

'Hold your horses. So far, they've gone in, and if you take a look with your binoculars, you'll see most of them are mingling round the main bar area. You can see through that big window. I saw a dining room behind that when I was scouting round, so I reckon they're going to eat first and then they'll get up to whatever. We're okay out here until it's dark. I'm not sure you're going to need your outfit as I think we might just move about discreetly instead. Do you see any hotel staff?' Susan shakes her head. 'Exactly. He's emptied the place, the owner.

Whatever they're up to isn't going to be normal fare.'

When we see them leave the main lobby and bar, we skirt around the outsides of the hotel. Looking in the rear, we can see them in the dining hall, but there's no service. They're all walking up and getting their own meal, served from plated silver canteens, possibly made up earlier on in the day. I've a bet that they'll just leave all the dishes to go off to do what they do, and the hotel staff will pick everything up in the morning. I have to admit, if I were a member of that staff, I'd be dead keen to know what's going on. What owner in their right mind just sends his staff home when you've got guests coming?

Dinner is served. Once everyone's finished, the night starts to crawl in. I tell Susan to stay where she is, watching with the binoculars, and I sneak up closer, perching myself at a window. I'm able to look inside, and I doubt anyone can see me. The noise inside is deafening until someone strikes a glass and the room falls silent. It's hard to hear what's going on as the glass muffles everything. But then I see someone I missed before. Laura Sutherland's in there, and she's cutting quite a figure with it.

There's a man at the front, possibly the hotel owner, who looks like he's introducing certain people. I watch Alison Hadleigh stand up and move to the front of the hall. Then Laura comes as well. They look at each other and then disappear. The man continues to explain things until the two women return, dressed in priestess outfits. It's like a large monk's habit, all in white, but on their head they've antlers, in some sort of bizarre head gear.

I have absolutely no idea what's going on, but I watch as, one by one, everyone walks to the front and is picked to go to either side. There seems to be no discrimination between men and women, each just told to stand in a group beside either Laura or Alison. And then everyone disappears off except for the two women and the man hosting. I can't hear what's going on, but words are exchanged between the two women, and at one point they step close, hands being placed on shoulders. Then there's a slap, a slap back, and a man stepping in between. It's quite a bizarre sight as the antlers on the head gear clash as well, nearly pulling one off.

There's still a tête-à-tête and a fair bit of tension as people return to the room. They're now dressed in their own monks' habit and I feel like I'm on a rather bad movie set from a 1970s horror film. Soon they disappear, one group following Laura out of one door, and the other group following Alison Hadleigh out of the other. The man also follows Alison Hadleigh.

With that I route back to Susan but I'm not quite sure what to tell her, and I begin to wonder just how much she's seen of the world. But the last thing I need is her being shocked, and so I say to her that she's probably going to see some quite strange action tonight, and describe exactly what everyone was wearing, with a warning that underneath they might be wearing something very, very different.

I tell Susan to put on her balaclava and we make our way to the door. I pick the lock which is not difficult to open it. Once inside, I listen intently but there's no noise on the ground floor. So, we climb the stairs slowly. There's a light on. I take Susan in hand and we walk down a corridor of rooms. Single doors, like any hotel. We stop outside the first one and inside we can hear noises. One by one, we walk down, listening, and each time finding the same sounds, the sounds usually described as adult sports. Susan is a bit agog at what's happening, and I don't blame her. I am too, but I still have my senses on edge.

When I hear a door open, I pull her aside with me into a cupboard I've spied in the hallway. Inside are cleaning fluids, but there's just about enough room for us. I close the door, pushing her back against one wall and with me sitting against the other. Clearly there's going to be no need for anybody cleaning tonight, but given what's going on, who can tell? So, I make sure I'm ready in case somebody opens the door.

There's a lot of laughter in the hall, and the noise of about ten or fifteen people walking along. There's a lot of explicit descriptions about what people have just been doing, and certainly I'm hearing some things that I've never thought of, but as the sound dies down, I gently open the door. Looking towards the far end of the hallway, back towards the stairs, I see a pair of hairy buttocks disappear around the corner. It's not the sight I was hoping for.

Quickly, I step out and listen again to see if anyone else is about. Some of the doors are open in the rooms. Indicating for Susan to follow me, we step inside one. There are some ropes hanging from the wall and the bedsheets are in a mess. On the floor there are some devices I don't recognize and, quite frankly, I don't want to recognize, but it all looks like sport. Some would say harmless fun, but it's not my sort of fun.

After a quick look around, my suspicions are confirmed and the reason for being here tonight has gone. So, I tell Susan we need to head back out before everyone comes back up the stairs. As we reach the end of the corridor, there's a hubbub going on down below and I believe everyone must be back in the hall. Whether they're getting picked again for a second round or whatever's going to happen, I don't really care, but instead race down the stairs.

I unlock the door, close it over, but as I'm putting the lock back into place, people start moving again from the main hall and I have to duck behind a wall until they pass. Once again, it's the same hubbub, the same type of discussions.

Once everyone is upstairs, I make my way back to the hedgerows with Susan, and we walk round slowly until we find our car at some distance. Only then do I take the balaclava off, and Susan hers, as we sit in the car.

'What the hell was all that?' she says. 'There was loads of them from the golf club. Did you get a look at them, Paddy, as they went up the stairs?'

'No,' I say. 'We were hiding. You should have been round the corner. There was no need to look. No need to find out.'

'But I had to,' she said. 'I'll never be able to look at our captain again. He was just wearing one of those . . . well, it must've been painful.' And then she starts to laugh. 'It's so ridiculous,' she says. 'One of them, he just looked so ridiculous. And you said it was like monks' outfits. Nobody was wearing any monks' outfits. Why would they bother with the monks' outfits?'

'Maybe they didn't want to know what everybody was wearing to start off with. Maybe that was part of the shock. Maybe that was part of the game.'

She looks at me. 'Have you been to these things before?'

I'm a little bit mortified that she even thinks that I would attend something like this, a girl who was showing infatuation a couple of days ago. 'No,' I say. 'But it stands to reason, doesn't it? Why bother with all the elaborate nonsense? You need to think things through sometimes. It's what part of being an investigator's about,' and I look out of the window. I hope she's buying that and that she seriously doesn't think I attend these things.

We drive off until we find a decent place to stop. I quickly change into more normal clothing. Back in the car, Susan is silent. She's not annoyed, she just seems contemplative. When we get to the house, I drop her off, and she stands for a moment and then, as if having an epiphany, she turns, and she looks at me. 'Paddy, how on earth am I meant to play golf with these people again?'

Chapter 17

As I pull away from Susan's with haste, I get a text on my phone. You shouldn't look at these things when you're driving, but I do. And it's from Maggie. She's offering me a bed to sleep off the night's activities. And let me get it clear—she's not offering me her bed. I don't think she's like that but I'm a little bit tempted. No, in honesty, I'm more than tempted, but business is not concluded tonight. So, I pull over and text her back, asking if she wants to grab a coffee tomorrow afternoon. When she says yes, I continue my drive and I'll admit I'm pretty happy. But like I say, the night's not over yet.

I get to Alison Hadleigh's, parking some distance away and then sneaking in through the back. She's not home when I get in, but I do at least have the code. I grab a shower and get changed for bed. Lying there, I ponder on what's happened that night. It seems our Alison is a woman with a lot of appetites, but in fairness, they all seem legal. Everyone was volunteering to be there and doing it of their own free will. It was just the spat she had with Laura that made me wonder. I might drop Laura's name in and find out a bit more about her. Maybe it's time to push Alison. I weigh the options, wondering whether or not to come clean with my client and find out what's going on. The problem with that often is the client decides to act and at this point in time, that could be a bad thing. Her husband's alive, but if the whole shebang gets closed down that he's involved in, whatever that exactly is, he can end up getting disposed of in the same way that our Mr Porterfield was. That's what's strange as well. Nobody has said he's missing yet. If that's the case, what are the people that work for him being told? And who's told them? I won't find that out on Monday because I'm not there anymore. Certainly, there's been no gossip up at the golf club. Nobody's missed him. And I wonder if he even had a space. Maybe that's something for Susan to find out, keep her occupied. She'd be on a bit of a high after tonight's success.

I drop off, and then next thing I hear is a door being opened. But the room I'm in is bright, making me wonder if I left the light on, but I didn't. It's simply the sun shining through the curtains. I check my clock. Six in the morning. Must be Alison.

I begin to understand how long these evenings she's involved in go on. I guess it would be a quiet Sunday in front of the box today. I hear her fumble around, enter the bathroom and then retch, being sick down the toilet. I guess there's a lot of alcohol at these things as well.

My phone beeps and it's Martha with some more detail. She says the shipments are definitely coming on Sunday, but they won't be arriving until at least eight o'clock that night. She provides evidence for this with some shipping documents and some transactions that have been placed across different countries. She's intercepted the odd email as well. Martha's good—incredibly good—and nobody really even knows about her. In the old days you had the force. You could phone people; you were the police. You could do things and you could ask for computer help from a whole department. But today, being out on my own, I need somebody like Martha and in fairness, she'll pick up a good fat cheque from this because I don't come that cheap.

I'm kind of glad that it's going to be later tonight because I wanted to meet Maggie and I know what was said last night and what it means for her. The coffee this afternoon is also an excuse to find Susan and make sure she isn't coming because after yesterday she'll be beaming for another bit of covert action. But this one won't be as easy to talk your way out of if it goes to pot.

Alison's retching brings me back to my senses and I wonder, should I get up and see if she's all right? But then I hear a thump from the bathroom door and some water being gargled, before my own bedroom door opens and there stands, not exactly in her glory but more like somebody that's been pulled through a hedge backwards, Alison Hadleigh. She's got those hungry eyes, but she also looks as if she might fall over at any minute.

'I hope you got a taxi back,' I say. 'It looks like it was a heck of a night.'

'Of course, I got a taxi. I'm always sensible when I drink and yes, for your information,' she says, and sweeps her hair to one side with what's meant to look like a movie star flick, but what ends up looking like a tired, old comment. She rocks slightly and hits the wall.

'It looks like too much of a night,' I say. 'You could do with going to bed.'

'You're probably right. Yes, I could, Paddy,' she says and stumbles forward to my bed. 'I could do with going to bed with you, Paddy,'

Oh heck, here we go. I step out of the bed, reach for my dressing gown because I'm dressed in boxer shorts, and put it on quickly. I come round to the other side of my bed where she's now lying, arms draped everywhere.

'Get me out of my dress, Paddy. Let's go to bed.' I reached down, grab her arm, pull her forward. It's not easy without another arm to get someone to their feet, but my right arm's strong these days and I soon swing it round behind her shoulders, pulling her upwards. I have to put my arm then round her waist to try and walk her forward. As we reach her bedroom door, it's an awkward mess, as we have to turn sideways to get both of us through it. She collapses into me, arms around my shoulders.

'Come on, Paddy. You know where we want to go,' and she plants herself, both lips, firmly on mine. I shut mine tight and she seems somewhat disappointed.

'You're no fun,' she said. 'I had lots of fun last night. You could have been fun.' There's going to be no information from her this morning, but I manage to dance her right into her bedroom, where somehow, she seems to hold herself upright. 'Take my dress off, Paddy. Get me ready for bed.'

I think this is a ploy, but I decided to play the straight man and asked her where her nightgown is. 'I don't wear a nightgown,' she says. 'I don't sleep in anything.' I reach out to her back for the zip on her dress. But it's been worked so often, it's caught. So, I have to lean forward with my teeth holding on and then pull the dress back down. I move quickly, drop it over Alison's shoulder, let it go to the floor, and then we start to talk about removing other things. I put my hand in the small of her back, push her forward gently, and she falls onto the bed.

'Call me when you're sober,' I say and walk out of the room. It's about five minutes later when the snores begin. She's no use to me in this state and I think if I go back to bed and she wakes up, she could be joining me. I pull on some clothes, jump in the car and go for a drive. It's Sunday so there are not a lot of places open but I find a fast burger joint that also does breakfast. As I was beginning to eat my pancakes with sticky maple sauce over the top, I get a text from Maggie asking what time she wants me to meet her this afternoon. I look outside the diner and it's quite a stunning morning. Cold, but stunning. I ask her if she's ready to jump in a car now.

She asks where on earth we're going to go on a Sunday morning and I tell her just to drive in, meet me in the diner, and not to get worked up about how she looks. It's only breakfast we're having. When she arrives, I see she's made little effort, as I asked. That's good because I don't think she needs a lot of work. Sometimes you find women who just seem to endlessly want to change their appearance. Pile on the makeup, make her eyebrows look like this, make her eyelashes look this way when in fact they looked great to begin with. Her hair's tied up at the back as well, so she hasn't even bothered with that. And she's in blue jeans and a plain grey jumper. In fact, she looks like she's about to go off and do the garden or paint the house.

'What did you do to my daughter last night?' She says. 'Three in the morning before she shut up about it.'

'Well, that's something else I'm going to have to teach her, how to keep her mouth shut after an op.' Maggie laughs and slides in beside me. 'Any loose pancakes going free?' she says. I give her a plastic fork, lift it up to her mouth, and she chews it thoughtfully before turning to me and saying, 'Not exactly the best, is it?'

'Keep your voice down. People in here work awfully hard,' I say.

'Come on and get in the car,' she says. 'Let's do this properly.'

I find that properly is sitting on a beach with a packet of four croissants from the local supermarket and two take-away coffees. We perch on a rock, looking at the sea and for the first ten minutes, we simply eat and drink.

'I like the sea,' says Maggie suddenly. 'I always wanted to get a boat, go up and down this west coast. You ever want it to be a sailor, Paddy?' she says.

'I am a sailor,' I say and see the look on her face. 'Unfortunately, my boat's having a little bit of work done to it down at the harbour.'

'Really? What is she?'

'She's just a small yacht,' I say. 'It's fairly compact but it's where I live. In my business, I tend not to have too many roots.' And this seems to sadden her. 'I'm not lying to you, either,' I say. 'I don't really have many relationships. I've had people pass through for a couple of weeks, but if I get too close, sometimes they get hurt. It's one of the things with your daughter; I need to keep her away from certain elements. Even in this case. Last night was an easy stakeout and if we got caught, we could explain our way out of it. Nobody was going to get hurt but there's other times she won't be coming with me for a long time.'

'Good,' says Maggie, 'but shut up about her. Tell me about your boat.'

I spent the next hour telling her all about Craigantlet, where I have sailed in her, where I've moored, what she's like inside. When I finish speaking, Maggie simply nods and looks out to the sea. 'Do you think you'd have a room for a second person on board?' she asks. 'Maybe not long term, maybe short term. Every once in a while.'

'Possibly,' I say. 'Very possibly. But you know what I am. And I'm guessing it doesn't scare you that much because you're letting your daughter get involved.'

'Told you before, stop talking about her. Her business with you is her business. That's her path she wants to follow and that's the way she is. Just look after her. But as for me, I'm looking for a different path.'

I stand up. 'Come on,' I say, 'let's take a dander.' The dander, or a short walk if you're not from home, turns into an hour and a half's saunter up and down the beach, looking at the water, the tide slowly moving its way out. We're surrounded by seagulls squawking, but otherwise it's just a quiet lap. And for the first time in a week, I feel at ease.

She tells me about the soldier she married and of his untimely death. About raising two girls on her own and how it may be her time of life now that they're growing up. And she tells me about a love of the sea and coming down here to the beach several times a week. And I tell her what happened with me. About losing my arm and about starting up again.

We make our way back to the car eventually where, sitting inside, she turns to me and says, 'So, where do we go from here?' I know a lot of women who would have pushed me for something very quickly, but she seems happy just being in my company.

'I need to get this case sorted, Maggie. Okay? And then we go to that cinema.'

'And you'll show me your boat, won't you?' she says. I hesitate slightly. 'I mean you'll show me your boat out on the water. Not the bunk at the back of it,' she says. 'It's been a long while, Paddy, so we do this slowly.' I nod. 'And I know I said I wouldn't bring it up,' she says. 'But if my daughter's involved with your business, I want to make sure you and I are right because I don't want that screwing up her life.'

I sit back in the car seat and look at her. 'That works for me,' I say. But, actually, inside it doesn't. I'm really taken by this woman and it's only business that's keeping me from looking to push faster, but I hear myself say, *Don't wreck this one, Paddy.* I'm usually a rather good judge of character and she's a character I want to get to know better.

We drive back to her house where Susan seems to be up and about.

'So, when are we heading off on the stakeout?' Susan asks.

'I told you last time, you're not going on this one—It's too risky. You stay put and I'll tell you all about it when I come back.'

'When we come back home,' she says.

'Stop the arguing,' I say. 'You're working for me; it's not professional. I call the shots, you follow them. That's all there is to it, nothing personal, nothing angry. It's just what is.'

And I don't pay much more attention than that because Maggie's made a coffee. We sit and we drink some more but I haven't even had the heart yet to tell her I prefer tea. I get one of her smiles again, as I leave driving off the road. I find it hard to switch off, hop back to the job, but I have to, because this one is dangerous.

Arriving back at Alison Hadleigh's, I grab some gear and then find Alison in the front room. She's sitting in a large dressing gown, not the normal one she swans around in, wrapped up tight. As I walk into the room, she makes no effort to make a pass at me, just merely lies there, holding her head. She's white and I reckon she's probably been sick a few more times.

'Heck of a rough night,' I say. 'You all right? Can I get you anything?'

'You probably have to go,' she says. 'Just let me die. Talk to me tomorrow about things.'

'Okay, I'll be out tonight,' and I tell her I probably will have some more information by the morning, but she doesn't seem to care. I reckon I could be a masked burglar walking in here and she would just tell me to take what I want. Just as long as I didn't bother her.

With that, I take my leave, get geared up in my car and drive out. Finding again that carpark for the forest that's just along from the farm we visited before, I noticed quite a large contingent of his goons around. I'm using false number plates on the car and pull a few knickknacks out from the bag to hang around the rear-view mirror and put on the dashboard, just things to make sure they know it's a different car. I nestle down in the woods, dressed this time in green and brown, like some sort of sniper, except I've got a camera with me instead of a rifle. It's got a good telescoping lens on it and I'm soon clicking away, picking up people walking back and forward. There's a number of goons dressed as usual in their black way, wearing sunglasses for some reason, even though it's not that warm a day.

The minibus pulls up with twenty people inside. I photograph them all stepping out. They seem sombre, not like people happily off to work and certainly not doing the seven dwarfs' song. There are a few more cars pulling up and people getting out. They don't look like they're there for protection but are there to supervise and run operations. Then a car pulls up with Laura Sutherland in it. She's accompanied by Sergei and they march off to the main building.

About an hour later, a truck turns up just as the light's beginning to fade. There are no lights on in the building, but as the truck pulls in and goes around to the far side of the farm, I see some large barn doors open in the place where all the tables were before. They start unloading from the back, so I start photographing and watch. Once everything is unloaded, the truck pulls away. The doors of the farmhouse are shut and for all intents and purposes, the farm looks shut down.

There are still regular patrols, the men in black walking around. But as I'm photographing one, I see there's something in the undergrowth. A person is completely dressed in black. They've got a balaclava on and are creeping along through the undergrowth, but it's not being conducted in a very discreet way. In fact, they're quite lucky because whoever it is seems to be walking round in between the guards. However, I doubt this has been a deliberate action. I turn my camera on this person, look at the rough size and I think I know who it is. And then she takes the balaclava off, so that even without the camera, I see the red ponytail on the young face.

What the hell is Susan doing here?

Chapter 18

There's an anger building up in me, and I know I need to control it. There's no point in losing my cool at this point as I could blow my cover as well as hers. Waiting for another guard to pass before moving around the hedgerows, I approach Susan from the rear. She's crouched down, but anyone can spot her easily from behind. Even from the front, I don't think she's that inconspicuous. She's certainly too focused on what's in front of her and not looking around. Yes, I've got experience of approaching people, people that I don't want to see me, but this is so easy it's unbelievable. Stepping up behind her, I put an arm around and cover her mouth with my hand, pull her back, and say, 'Don't move. It's me. Don't speak. Just turn around slowly.'

She does this and she's looking up at me with accusing eyes, eyes that say, 'What the hell are you doing?' If she looked at my eyes, she'd see the same question coming right back at her. But this is not the place for a row. We need to have that discussion somewhere else. I've got some photographs, but I'll need to move further in, see if I can get close, but not with Susan. Maybe it was a mistake taking her last night. Maybe it was just making her run before she's ready to walk. I march us further back until I see a small copse of trees and take us inside of them. There's good cover from all sides here. Sitting down, I get her to face me, hold a finger up to my mouth, then address her in very hushed tones.

'You were told to stay home. This is no place for you.'

'I came last night. You can't keep me out of the big stuff,' she says. 'This is where it's all going down. You can solve this here tonight.'

'I can solve nothing. I'm here simply to get photos, photograph it all, evidence, something I can hand over to somebody else, and that requires me to tiptoe around. Something I've learnt over the years, not something I ran out at eighteen and did straight away. You stay here tonight, and you will get caught. These people aren't some sort of clown fraternity who like dressing up and getting off with each other. No, this is the real deal. These are nasty people and they may even take you to a field and put a gun in the back of your head. You're going home.'

She's playing the puppy dog eyes. I can see I hurt her feelings, but frankly, I don't care, as long as she goes home, 'Where's your car?' I ask.

'In the car park. The one we used before.'

'On the bright side. If we got caught together, we can always say we're having another rendezvous.' After I've said it, I realize that was a mistake, because her eyes have lit up as if I've given some credence to why she's here. Some sort of small alliance that means she can stay. 'We won't need it,' I say, 'because you're going home, and when I'm finished with here, we're going to have a proper conversation. If you work for me you learn to follow what's been said, you learn to take instruction. You don't freelance. Freelancing gets people killed,' but I'm not sure she's even listening. The head's turned away, there's possibly even a few tears in those eyes, but I can't let up at this point—she needs to go.

'Make your way back,' I say, 'Make your way back. I'll make sure you're safe there. Now. Go, while I've still got time to get back and get my photographs.' With that, she trudges off. There shouldn't be anybody this far out skirting the grounds, but I tail her back to the car park anyway, and watch as she gets into the car. Once inside, she stops for a moment. She's got her head in her hands and she's crying. It's breaking me up inside to see her that way, because she's been such a great kid. Found out so much for me, helped me, but this is big stuff and she can't be involved.

As soon as I see her drive off and turn down the country lane out of here, I return quickly to my previous vantage point. They won't be packing clothing too quickly. I reckon it'll take them most of the night, and so I sit down for the long haul, waiting for my opportunity when everyone gets a little bit sleepier. The farm buildings, as I recall, have all the production down at one end and then through into the smaller buildings is where Sergei and Laura were meeting. That's where they'll be again.

I'd quite like to get some photographs of the pair together so I skirt further around until I see a light coming from one of the buildings. It's at the far end, behind some curtains, but it looks like the room they used before. If I'm lucky, they'll look out at some point. I start climbing a tree. It's nice and sturdy and I'm able to get up into the branches to then point my camera straight at the window. I bed myself down in the tree because this could be a long stint, but if I can get that photograph of the two of them together deep in conversation in the building, it'll certainly help my case.

It's about two hours later when Laura comes out the front. She's smoking a cigarette. I don't remember her ever having smoke on her breath or on her clothes when we played golf. Maybe she's just nervous. I capture some shots of her standing there, but it's not Sergei. She returns inside and he appears a half hour later taking fresh air by the looks of it. I capture some shots of him, but they're not together. Then before he steps inside, I see Laura pull back the curtains and I photograph her through the window. He's on the move back up and I see an angry row as he enters. I fire off shots on the camera like there's no tomorrow, and I maybe get forty seconds of the two of them in the room at different angles before he storms across and shuts the curtains. He knows his business, but she doesn't. At least not to his level.

With the preferred image captured, I climb back down the tree, listening intently to the sounds of the night. Out in the countryside, there's plenty of noise. Animals moving in the dark, cries out to the night, but they're all very restful, if you're used to them. The noises that are there above that, of someone walking around, a guard passing by, the quiet hum of people packing inside a locked building—there's what's different.

It's time to get inside the building. I scurry back to my car, leaving my large camera behind, and taking with me a ridiculously small one. It can go on the end of a stick, meaning I can photograph around corners. It gives me an image without being seen, and the small TV screen at the end of the stick allows me to know what I'm looking at. There's no need to snap away, it just constantly records. The night's drawn in properly now, and it's two in the morning, which is good because fatigue will be setting in with people. That's when they get lax, when it's easier to move about. Hiding in my hedgerow across from the farmhouse, I watch the guards pass again, and see how easy they have become. On their first watches they were looking everywhere, now they're just walking, eyes scouting less, and the timing between patrols is becoming erratic and longer.

I step lightly across the farmyard and it's easy to tell how disused it is, because there's no animal muck of any sort. There's a door at the rear that the guards have been using for coming in and out, and if I've timed it right there'll be nobody going through there for the next five minutes. As I approach, I listen intently. No one there. Open the door. Step inside.

To my right are the run of corridors up to the large barn I was in previously. To the left are the rest of the farmhouses where the guards are hanging out. I doubt they'll be sleeping, but some will definitely be taking a break, so I move towards the production end, quietly making my way up in the dark of the corridor until I see a door. At the bottom, light is coming through. I hear people swearing and cursing, and the accents are not from this country. Possibly migrants brought in, people trafficked, something like that. I take out the camera and I'm able to pop the thin end of it underneath the door, turning it slightly. It gives a reasonable picture inside. I can see maybe four or five supervisors, and people with hoodies on. Part of me thinks I could wait until someone comes out to go to the bathroom, overpower them and come back dressed as them. But I haven't got my prosthetic with me, so how do you explain losing an arm in the toilet?

Instead, I think about the windows on the side of the barn, they're all closed off with shutters and there's also the large doors at the far end. I think it's got a keyhole and if I can put the camera through there, I should be able to get a lot of good footage. That means standing outside while the guards come round. Not so easy but I'll not be able to go through this door.

As I'm pondering on this, I see someone walking towards the door, and pull the camera back quickly, stepping lightly back along the corridor. I walk through a door and realize it is the toilet, and spin around behind it, closing the door quickly. There are footsteps coming my way. As the door opens, I stay behind it. A light comes on. There's a man in a hoodie, which he pulls down as he walks towards the cubicle. There's two toilets here, two cubicles, and he takes up the first one, shutting the door behind him without even looking, which is a good job, because if he turned around properly, he'd have seen me, and I'd have had to take him out. I think about disappearing back out the door, but instead I quietly take the camera wire, place it gently over the top so it barely pushes past the top of the cubicle door. I get a good shot with a man sat there. He even looks up briefly but doesn't see anything before looking down

I've got an image of a face, and he's not a guard; in some ways he's probably an innocent. I can pass this on to the authorities, but he'll be coming back out soon, so I need to step out. I make my way back down the corridor to the door the guards have been using to come in and out. Checking my watch, I've probably got about two minutes before the next one passes. I make my way back across the farmyard, hide in the hedgerow, and watch as he moves with a saunter. As I said before, at the start of the night, everyone's sharp, but now the weariness has grown in and as he moves past in a sluggish fashion, he's not even looking towards me.

Once he's clear, I step back onto the courtyard, go along the side of the building behind the guard until I reach those large barn doors. Here, I stick the camera through the keyhole. I know I've got probably five minutes, at best. The image is a bit of a fish lens, but I'm able to twist it here and there, and I can see people packing, guards stood around. If you look closely, you can see the bulge of the guns that they're holding inside their jackets. There's nothing discreet about this, it's simply good old-fashioned forced labour. There are some men in scabby jeans, t-shirts, jumpers, and a few women as well. One of the guards is looking at some of the women, saying something in Russian. I'm not sure if they understand, because if they did, they'd be deeply offended. Not that my Russian is up to that much.

There's a thought inside me, that I could release these people, but really, I'm not quite sure how that would pan out. I could blow the whistle on this, but what would it do for the judge? Five minutes later, I'm expecting the next guard, so I pull my camera away, tuck it back inside my jacket and move back to the hedgerow. The guard's late this time, by about three minutes, but at least he's there, and he's passed me.

Then there's a cry, and the guard turns and runs back along the farmyard, right towards the far end. There's a lot of noise, chatter in Russian, and I race along as best I can. Tonight's a dark one, clouds overhead and the moon's not giving a lot of light, but I can see three or four figures now. They've hit someone, pulling at them as they're on the ground. I wonder what's going on. Then I get a deep, sinking feeling.

She couldn't have been so dumb to come back, surely not, and yet I know it. Something inside me tells me that she's come back. She's tenacious, but she's also very green at the moment. Too green. The look in her eyes as she left me, I should have caught it. That moment when she was saying to herself, *I'll prove to him. I'll show him.* That initial infatuation that's changed into making me a figure she wants to emulate, live up to, something that doesn't work in this game. This game where you live in the moment, judge each second, and keep yourself safe. Otherwise, it could be your last.

I could jump out, run over and try and take on four guys, but frankly, it's not going to work. They've also got guns, which I haven't, because I can't stand the things, bringing them only when necessary. Tonight, until this happened, it wasn't necessary. They drag her away towards the farmhouse building and I race through the undergrowth to keep eyes on her. They'll come out and search for me soon, which doesn't bother me, I'll be able to keep safe. What bothers me is how I'm going to get her back out of here.

My mind's racing, scrambling with how I keep her alive. Why shouldn't they just take her away and dispose of her? Stupid girl! I watch as they enter the farmhouse and I know where they're taking her, straight up to that room at the top. Straight up to Sergei, and Laura. Of course, they'll recognize her. They played golf with her, and that'll tag me into it as well. I was just going to sit here, and photograph the lorry coming back, taking the goods away, see how they're distributing them. But no, now I'm in full crisis mode as to how keep Susan alive.

She'll be up the stairs now, coming into the front room. Sure enough, the shadows are moving behind the curtains, the voices that were raised in a shout before are now quiet. Sergei will be taking charge. He might be threatening her, but I need to give him something to keep her alive. I think desperately. She'll have her phone on her. If I ring, it will give away that I'm here. That means that rescue is not going to happen. What do I have, I think? I've got a load of evidence, but that won't bother him, he'll just shut it down. He'll kill her anyway, come for me.

If I had the judge, this could play out differently. It's my bet that Laura's kept him hidden, kept him safe, unlike Angus Porterfield. If that's the case, she's invested in this as well with him. That could stir up problems between them, but it just might keep Susan safe until I can do a trade.

I take out my phone and dial Susan's number. It's put down, switched off. They must have taken it from her. Time to send a text. I punch in the words, 'We need to talk, Sergei. Need to talk, Laura, because your judge friend is in my grasp.' I wait to see if anyone comes out. Sure enough, the guards come out to start searching around. They know someone's watching now. I text again and tell him to take his goons back inside or the judge goes straight to the police, and a trade would be off. I know they've got my answer when thirty seconds later his men retreat back inside the building, and this time they're ringing me.

Chapter 19

'Sergei, harm her and the deal's off. I've got plenty that can bury you.' That's my first words before he's even spoken, because I know I have to get in quick. 'Bring her to the window so I know she's still safe.' There's a short wait and then the window's opened. Laura's standing there, holding Susan up, whose eyes are streaming, her face a mess. 'Good,' I say. 'I have the judge. I know he knows the whole operation. More than that, I know that he can identify you. I also have certain friends who can close you down and you'll never get out of the country. For now, keep treating her well.' I need to arrange where we're going to drop off our respective goods.

It's a bit of a gamble because I actually don't know exactly what's going on. I don't know all the relationships. Would he cut and run? Just kill off everyone and get out of the country? Drop everyone that's even been here? Who can tell? Or maybe he's got some issues himself, back home? I know Sergei and Laura were having problems, otherwise why is he coming after them? This seems like a lucrative business, but something's afoot and I need to know what. I'm thinking Laura's going to back me up, even just to keep her man alive, or for whatever reason she needs the judge.

'Well, my friend,' says Sergei, in his Russian tome, 'you do more than play good golf. Be in touch and do not worry. She will be safe, but when you come, I don't just want him, I want my money.'

'Then you'll need to give me a day or two to get that,' I say, trying to buy some time by which to work out what I'm doing.

'You call tonight, eight o'clock, and we talk, but if I smell anyone else coming after me, I won't hesitate. She'll get hurt. I think we understand each other.' he says, 'But why are you so daft bringing such a young one into this, and caught so easily? Maybe you didn't. Maybe she just likes you.'

I know what he's doing, trying to rack the guilt up on me. Susan's probably spilled the beans about it and that's why he's able to use it. Well, at this moment in time I've got a card he doesn't have, but I need to move quick. I don't know if Laura will buy it, and if she doesn't, she could nip there first, and warn the guard. I'm already making my way back to the car as I continue on the phone to Sergei, letting him know I know what operations are going on, that they're all involved. By the time the conversation has ended, I'm driving away, dialling my phone again. This is a conversation I'm not looking forward to, but it's one I need to have.

'Paddy, what time is it? What's wrong?'

'Maggie,' I say. My voice doesn't have its usual cool and calm because I'm about to give her some very grave news. 'Is Kirsten with you?' I ask.

'Yes, she's in the house. Why?'

'Pack a bag, both of you. I'm picking you up in five minutes. Do not make me wait. I'll explain everything but grab a bag. Be at the front of your house and be quick about it.'

'What's wrong?' she says, 'Is it Susan?' Not knowing Maggie

that well, I say, 'Bag. Front of house. You and Kirsten.'

It's only wise to pick them up because they're leverage now as well. If Sergei were to get hold of them, I could end up having to trade, and not under my own terms. He knows I probably don't care that much about the judge, which is incorrect. It's my client's husband. The plan is still to get him back alive, but that might fade because Susan's become my number one priority.

The street's quiet as I drive down and park out in front of their house. Maggie's at the door and Kirsten's locking up behind her. They quickly get in. Kirsten in the back, Maggie in the front. As soon as she's inside, she's looking at me, tears in her eyes.

'What's wrong, Paddy? Where's Susan? She hasn't come home yet.'

'Nope. She hasn't. She turned up on the stakeout,' I say. 'I managed to intercept her, told her to go home, watched her drive away, but then she came back, and they've got her. She walked straight into it.'

'What the hell are you letting her do that for?' says Kirsten. Maggie put hand up.

'Not now, not now,' she says. 'Paddy's got a plan. He needs to have a plan. Let him work.'

That was an unexpected twist, but I knew I liked her. Not for her simple looks, but rather for her overall being. Her wisdom, her calmness, here in the midst of a child of hers facing death, she's still thoughtful.

'I've got to go and pick up a man,' I say to them, 'He won't like it and he's going in the boot, but there's another man guarding him. I'm just banking on the fact I can get to this guy before the man guarding him gets informed about what's going on.

I'll need you two to pull up in the car in front of the house, like you've been broken down. You need to freelance it. The guard will come up to you and I'll come in from behind him, but you need to put on a good show. Do you understand?' Maggie nods, but Kirsten's in a state in the back. 'Do you understand?' I insist, raising my voice slightly. 'This isn't the time to go to pieces, Kirsten. This is a time your sister needs you. Do you understand?'

'She'll be fine,' says Maggie, 'Leave it.' There's silence in the car and we drive on. As we get up to the road, I pull over, telling Maggie to step across and take the wheel. I invite Kirsten to get into the front and I get down low in the back. I tell them the house is around the next corner up on the left-hand side, where they should stop, close to the front of it.

'Pull in, get out and lift up the bonnet. There's a torch in the glove compartment. Pretend to look for something, have a spat while you're doing it.'

Lying in the back, it's all out of my hands. I wait until I hear the car come to a halt. The doors open and Maggie is sensible enough to leave hers ajar as she pops the boot. They start swearing at each other. It's almost comical, but then I hear a voice in the background. It's a Glasgow voice and it's asking what's wrong. It's not offering help, rather it's just looking to move them on. Then I hear him taking a phone call. The phone buzzing. Lifting it to his ear, and the word boss. I open the rear door, creep by around the side of the car. Maggie's begging at him, asking him to come back and look at the engine. She thinks something's wrong, but the man's waving a hand at her, turning away with some agitation. I've got an iron bar from my car. It's a small one, but as I walk up behind him, I hear Kirsten, begin to shriek with fear. Luckily enough, I'm close enough to the man. As he turns, I'm able to club him across the back of the head. He falls to the ground. I grab his collar and I start pulling him.

'Give me a hand. Get him into the boot. He's out cold. There's some wire in the boot.' We start to tie him up and it's quicker than normal for me because Maggie's got two hands. I instruct her what to do and we then reverse the car up the drive of the judge's hideout. The man must be asleep as there's no lights on. I've broken into this house before and realize that the front door's got the latch on. I go to the back window, lift it up, step inside, and quietly make my way to the front door, undoing the latch and leaving the door open. Maggie comes in with me, but Kirsten is still in the car.

'Get her in,' I say, 'She can give us a hand.'

Maggie shakes her head, 'Just leave her. We can manage this. She's not like me, and she's not like her sister. Let me manage her. You do what you have to do.' We make our way to the man's bedroom and see him lying, snoring. I grab one of his arms and twist it hard. As he wakes up not knowing why he's in pain, he starts to shout. I'm not worried, as we're far from anyone. I'm driving his arm up, forcing him to turn over. Maggie's grabbing his other arm and as she pulls them together, she uses some handcuffs from the car. I tell her to go and look in the kitchen for tape or something similar. She comes back with that thick carpet stuff. Two minutes later, it's across his mouth.

In reality, he's fairly compliant. We take him outside where he stands while I pull the big man out of the boot and we tape the Glaswegian up. Once we put the judge into the boot and have closed it, we move the other man back into the house. Soon we're back outside, the judge in our boot, Maggie and

Kirsten with me, and we're driving off along the coast.

This is where I'm stuck. Where do I go now? I also need a new car because this one is known. It's five o'clock now and I drive out of town, heading up towards Ayr. When we get to the outskirts, I swap over and tell Maggie to drive. She drops me at the car rental which is only just beginning to open, and I tell her to drive further along and park up on the road on the way. I join her about half an hour later and together we disappear into the countryside, where we park my original car out of the way in a small layby. We take our judge and put him in the new boot. We check and his eyes are still wide open.

I pull into McDonald's and pick up some food. Then we sit, having breakfast looking out at the fresh morning. The clouds are rolling back and it's a brighter day, but the mood's very sombre. Standing up, Maggie turns to me.

'Can we get her? Are you sure we can get her back?'

I nod. 'I'll get her back, but we have to play it right. You need to trust me. If we go to the police now, she'll be dead. They'll kill off everyone. At the moment I think they can be dealt with, but I'm not sure of all the pieces, so I need another meeting with someone else and then I'll work at how I can play this.'

Maggie reaches over, putting her hand on my shoulder. 'Get her back for me,' she says, 'get her back. If you need me to do anything, you just say.'

I nod and think about what's next. We need somewhere to hide out. I pose the question, 'Does anybody have a friend or anything? Somewhere we can go. Somewhere we can lie low?' It's then that Kirsten looks up at me. Her eyes are watery. I'm not sure she's coping that well.

'My boyfriend's parents have a caravan. It's out on its own, and there's no one there this week. I've got a separate key because sometimes,' and here she looks at her mother, 'we go up there.' That seems like a hard revelation. I watch the pair of them, as Maggie simply nods.

'It's okay, dear. It's not like I didn't know.' Kirsten looks up and I see a faint grin. It's not a smile, the situation's too serious for that, but at least there seems to be some sort of coming around to the circumstances from the young girl.

'Then we go there,' I say. 'How far outside Stranraer is it?'

'Twenty minutes,' she says. 'It's well off the beaten track.'

'Okay,' I say, 'that's where you're going to need to hole up while I go and do my work.' We set off as the day begins and the traffic starts to build up around Ayr. By midday, we're installed in our new abode, which has a stunning view down into Loch Ryan. The judge is lying on one of the beds, his arms tied, his mouth covered. I'm going to speak to him shortly, but first of all, Kirsten is taken to the other bedroom and told to go to sleep by her mother, before she joins me outside, looking at the view of Loch Ryan. She steps to my right-hand side, taking my hand with her left arm.

'The next forty-eight hours,' I say to her, 'it'll be touch and go. There are no guarantees, but I'll do everything I can. I should have been cleverer. I should've seen it in her eyes.'

'You wouldn't have stopped her. She's impetuous. Just the same as I was back then. You can't blame her,' says Maggie; 'it's only the years that seasoned me, but go get her for me. Whatever it takes, Paddy, go get her for me.'

Chapter 20

We spend a lot of time simply looking at each other as we walk around the caravan, waiting for a move; waiting for someone to speak. Maggie's waiting for me to pick up a phone and call Sergei but I need to keep him waiting, mainly because I think someone else is going to call me first. As I said, there's a whole lot of waiting.

Thus, I'm standing out looking at the water when my mobile rings. It's a number I'm not sure of but I answer it anyway. 'Yes?' I say.

'If you want to work out how to keep her alive, you'll come and meet me.'

It's Laura's voice and she sounds deeply agitated. I wouldn't blame her. She's probably in this up to her neck and she's probably had an ultimatum. I half expected the call, a way of working out what's going on. In fact, I was banking on it. But I'm also not stupid enough to meet anywhere near here and so I arrange a meeting on the other side of Loch Ryan, down by the beach, somewhere nice and open; somewhere plenty of people can see us but still remote enough to have a proper discussion. I tell her I'll be there in two hours' time. It'll be the middle of the afternoon.

As I come off the phone, Maggie looks at me expectantly.

'It's Laura,' I say, 'she's looking to bargain; looking to make some sort of a deal.'

'Do you trust her?' says Maggie.

'Of course not, but she's got a lot to lose so I'll hear her out. At the moment, I'm struggling to see how we bring everybody in and still keep Susan alive. We may have to sacrifice justice on this one. Whatever happens, I'm getting Susan back.'

You can see the pain on Maggie's face. She really is struggling now. The reality of what's happened piling on her, but she steps forward and throws her arms around me, holding me tight. 'Just get her, Paddy. I don't care about the rest. Just get her. And as for this piece of shit behind me and the caravan, I don't care what happens to him. Just get my daughter.'

As much as I'm inclined to agree with her, I also realize that 'that piece of shit' as she puts it, is also my paycheque. Quite how Alison Hadleigh's going to take all this, I don't know, and I really wonder if she understands what her husband's involved in. Alison Hadleigh's life just seems to be about one party after another and not normal parties either. She seems to want to bed everything . . . but this judge, he's somehow different.

And with that, I step back into the caravan, closing the door behind me, making sure that Maggie and Kirsten are both outside. I take the tape off his face as he sits on the bed, hands tied behind his back, ankles strapped together.

'You should be rescuing me. You should be taking me away. My wife hired you, didn't she? You're the investigator. The one-armed one.'

'Well, I can't really deny the lack of an arm, can I?' I say. 'I was wondering how your wife got my name. It was you all along, so you must've known something was coming up; something was falling apart.'

He's sweating, his eyes becoming bulbous.

'These guys don't piss about,' he says, 'they'll kill me, they'll kill her, and they'll kill you. They'll wipe us all out.'

'What did you take?' I ask. 'What is it that you've got that they've come after?'

'Money. What do you think? It's money.'

I walk to the far end of the caravan and start to boil a kettle. He's still within earshot and I shoot back with, 'You got tangled up in the business with them, didn't you? Was it Laura that got you into that?'

'Yes,' he says, 'we did proper garments once upon a time. We were legit all the way for our trademark, everything coming from suppliers we knew. But she says, "We can make a fortune." She continues, "You've got a Russian connection and they'll bring their stuff in, proper trademarks and Fairtrade signs, all of it." But as soon as I got it, I could tell it wasn't. But Angus, he says, "We need to do it because the business isn't making enough money." And in the space of six months, we go from losing money hand over fist, to suddenly actually making significant profit.'

'So, what was the problem? Why are they after you?' I say. 'Hand in the till, was it?'

'They said they wanted a cut and at first it was reasonable, twenty percent, but then they just demanded more. They did it through Laura and we gave them thirty, and then we gave them fifty, and then after that, I'd had enough. We were running this business and running it hard, putting in all the work. Angus, in particular was pissed off with them and he says to me, "Let's start dropping the profits down. Let's start squirreling away, hiding it, and just tell them that we're running badly. I thought it was a good idea, but then they weren't interested. They wanted it anyway, told us we should do better. But each time we steered them off, Laura would put up a front and she'd say to them, the money isn't there. The only thing was, it was still coming in. And so, Angus hid it; put it away.'

'What, in an offshore?'

'No' says the man, incredulously. 'He put it away—hid it away inside a barn, just to be safe. The Russians checked; you see. They went through our accounts and through what we deposited into the banks, but they couldn't find it. But they're savvy bastards. They could tell from the accounts. They could tell from what we'd sold and what we were still demanding of them. They knew the money was there. I told Angus this, told him to say so and just pay them. But he didn't and then he disappeared.'

'And so, you decided to disappear as well. But you didn't tell your wife?'

'No,' he says. 'I knew I had to keep her out of it, so I just didn't turn up to play John Carson and I hid. I knew she'd call you. I knew she'd get an investigator on it. And lo and behold, here you are. But it's all a bit screwed up, isn't it? I overheard you. They've got that girl, whoever she is, the woman's daughter.'

'Yes, they have,' I say, 'and we're getting her back.'

'That's not your concern,' he says and tries to sit up on the bed, but I push him back down with my arm.

"'Sit there' I say and walk to the far end of the caravan where the kettle's boiled. Pouring myself a cup, I bring it back. I can see him looking with parched eyes, tongue hanging out.

'I could do with a cuppa,' he says.

'Just sit there and shut up. I need to think how we do this.' But he doesn't give me a chance. Instead, he starts gassing again.

'Don't trust Laura. Don't trust her at all. She's liable to just cut and run, leave me hung out to dry. I'm sure she dropped it about Angus. Sergei must have shaken her down to where he was. She said to me that they cut the body up, told me they put it in behind the twelfth hole in that hut. That's why I couldn't play with John Carson. That's why I wouldn't go near the club.'

'How long have you known her?' I say. 'How long have you known Laura?'

'Met her fifteen years ago at the golf club. We started playing around together. Got to know each other quite well.'

'Through the extracurricular activities, you mean,' I say. 'I managed to catch one of those outings.' I raise my eyebrows as I say it and he soon understands my meaning. 'Your missus and her don't get on very well, do they?'

He shakes his head, acting as if he's had an amount of misfortune. 'They both want to dominate,' he says, 'take control of it. I'm sure you saw them dressed up.'

I shake my head. 'I didn't get that close,' I say, 'kept a discrete distance. Not my cup of tea.'

'She likes to dominate; likes to control men, does Alison, and so does Laura. I used to love it,' he says. 'And we'd swap about. But Alison got jealous and then Laura got jealous back and there were some blazing rows, and outright fights. That's why Alison knows nothing about the business, not that she cares where the money comes from anyway. But Laura is always making herself get on top, so she'll cut me out of this and keep the business going. Don't trust her.'

'Don't worry,' I say. 'As long as we get the girl back first, I might save your ass, too; after all, you're my paycheque even if you have been up to the most stupid of stuff.'

The day is not as sunny as the previous ones and when I

reach the beach, it's overcast, a light drizzle starting to fall. But I see the car, its deep red colour matching the skirt that the woman wears as she climbs out of it. Laura's come dressed to impress, a smart blouse and jacket, the cut of them made to accentuate her body. Not that I care. I'm on my guard as I go to speak to her and the first thing I do is scan the area to see if I can see anyone. Sure enough, there's the big fellow that was outside the house.

'I see you brought company.'

'Just for my protection,' she says. 'He's also keeping an eye in case our friends are about. After all, we don't want them to see us talking, do we?'

'So how can I help you?' I ask. 'I think I've got something you want.'

'Don't play with us,' she says. 'They're baying for blood. Give me Russell. Give me Russell, you'll have the girl, and just walk away.'

'I'm not sure I can do that,' I say. 'Russell is actually my client. In some ways, I need to protect him more than anyone.'

'You can tell me that,' she says smiling, 'but really, you want the girl. I saw the way she looked at you when we played golf. I guess it's reciprocated. She's quite something for her age, isn't she?'

'She could also be my daughter so whatever you think is happening there, it's not. But I got her into this so I will get her out of it, one way or another. And understand,' I say, 'if that means you don't walk away, it doesn't bother me. I don't often threaten but when I do, I mean to carry it through. At the end of the day, if all else fails, I'll leave a trail of bodies and walk away. I might even do better than that and bury a lot of bodies and walk away. But those sorts of endings are messy and difficult to do, so I'm looking for a better one. So, what do you think, Laura? How do you see this ending? How do I end up with two people still alive and your Russians off our backs?'

'Tell Russell to give them the money. I can convince Sergei to take the money and let the girl go. Russell will just have to make a run for it. But you'll have to bring him with you. Sergei will want to see Russell and the money. He'll want both. If you do, he'll let Russell go. He'll hunt him down again, but you'll get your money and you'll be clear. You'll have the girl as well. It's not as if you give much of a damn about that judge.'

'You sure as hell don't, considering the two of you are closer than that. He says you used to play games together.' I raise my eyebrows, but she doesn't take any bait at all.

'Some of us can see that sort of thing as just sex. It's just what makes things fun. This is business and in a business sense, he burned his bridges—him with me, him and Angus Porterfield. Angus will be in the bottom of the sea soon if he hasn't made it there already, as someone that disappeared on a business trip; someone with his name disappearing overseas and not coming back. It'll be recorded as leaving the country on a private plane. There'll be no screams, nothing to log his face as he left. It'll be sad.

'But Alison, Russell's widow, won't care. She'll have a load of money. You might've seen her the other night. I'm assuming that's when you found out about my other activities. It's a pity you didn't join in.'

We stroll along the beach, the waves lapping the shore, seagulls shouting in the air. It's cool. I'm glad I've got my jacket on because the breeze is picking up, but she doesn't flinch, only taking her high heels off to stop the sand getting in amongst them.

'You could always just deliver him over, him and the money, walk away. I could probably let Sergei give you what, twenty percent? I'm sure he'd agree to that. And they'll never know anything beyond that. Keep it all quiet.'

'And what, he just lets me walk around knowing what's happening and what he's doing? Yeah, I'd be dead within a month and so would Susan. I'm not that naive. Tell him we're going to meet. We'll go somewhere out of the way. I'll send the place to him and there I'll have the judge, and I'll have the money, and he'll have Susan. I'll pass my packages over and he can pass his package back. And I'll have footage stored away of everything he's doing on records. I've been inside the business, Laura. I have both of you banged up to rights. It'll be stored online, somewhere to get dropped the minute anything happens to me or to her. And that's how it will work.'

'You're right. You can have the judge. The guy's played me anyway. Brought me into this to find things out; to solve it for him even though he ran and hid himself. Although he hid with your knowledge, didn't he? How'd you think this was going to work out? Did you think Sergei would just forget about it or are you just keeping your options open? Or do you really have some sort of feeling for the judge? I think you do. I think deep down you want him. He'd get Alison out of the way if he could. Deep down, when you met, you hit upon something because otherwise he'd be dead, like Angus Porterfield. You didn't feel anything for poor Angus, did you?'

In her defence, she barely reacts at all but instead turns and faces the sea. 'He was always too good to get rid of. That was the problem, you see. And she had her claws in him. You probably look at this stuff that we do and think we're just all sex-hungry, not interested in anyone. But she cares about him more than you know, and he for her because as much as he lets me entertain him, the one thing he wouldn't do was walk from her. And that's my angle. Bring him when we meet and tell him his only way out is with me. It's time to go make a new life.'

I don't see how that's going to work and I'm not quite sure what she means but if I'm handing him over to Sergei, where there's goons there, how is she going to extract him? How am I going to extract him? That's what's bothering me. And will she get in the way now? Will she try some half-assed effort?

I watch her walk away and I understand maybe some of what he sees in her. She's still loyal to him. She protected him. But he says she'll cut and run; she'll ditch him eventually. I think he's right. I think he's absolutely right because Sergei's probably put her on the line. Money back and him out of the way. Maybe this was her hope coming to me, seeing if I could solve it, dispose of Sergei, and Laura and Russel could just disappear off into the sun. Well, I'm not here to write fairy tales. I'm just here to get a young girl back and then maybe pick up my cheque if I can wrangle it.

As Laura drives away, my phone rings and I see from the tag it's Alison Hadleigh. Oh, well, twenty-four hours and she should know exactly what's going on. Let's hope she's still got a husband who's able to come home.

Chapter 21

Once I've left the beach, there's a call to Martha, to find out how she's going with the hacking of our group of Russians. I can see her pushing back on her glasses, giving me that look of, 'You have no idea how difficult this actually is,' before mentioning that she's managed to do it. She'll pull back the baggy sleeves on her sweater, as if it's a good day's work then mention that she's got the links. She's one of those people you never get to hear about, one of those people you never see. And she makes things happen that I haven't got a clue about. Moving money, hiding any transactions in the dark, breaking into bank accounts, especially these offshore ones. They're a mystery to me, but not to her.

And it was the first time I caught her that changed her life. She was ready to take millions, ready to go on the run with it, but she didn't understand the world she was getting into. I got her set right and I put her on contract. That's why she does what she's asked, every time. Just one of those workers that puts the extra effort in. And she's well worth her money.

The long and short of it is that once Sergei deposits the money, Martha's going to be able to put it into Sergei's personal account, not his bosses' account. That will make a big difference, because once they see it in his, they'll believe he's been playing them. I've seen this type of operation run before. The guys back at their office, they don't want anything to bother them. You run it and you deliver the money. It's exactly the same trick that Sergei is playing on Laura. You run the operation; you deliver the money. If it doesn't arrive then there's the consequences. And there'll be consequences for Sergei. If I can get the body of Angus Porterfield to turn up at the same time, that might be a bonus. But that one's out of my hands.

I arrive back at the caravan, where Maggie looks pleased to see me. She'd be hoping against hope that Susan was still alive, and I've got some simple plan, or it'll just be over. Beyond her, Kirsten looks more sceptical, or just giving me a much harder look. If Maggie weren't keeping her in check, she'd be beating into my chest with her hands, pummelling her fists in me, demanding her sister's return. I think Maggie's got a better idea how difficult that is. I just say my hellos and march into the caravan to find Russell Hadleigh again lying on the bed. I demand the money from him, demand to know where he's put it. And at first, he denies all knowledge, saying Laura is the one with it. This is crass and stupid because if Laura had the money, she'd simply hand it over. After all, that's what Sergei's looking for. Especially, as Laura still has that little something for Russell.

'And what if I give you it?' he says, 'What if I give up the money? You take it, you hand it over, you get your girl back, and I'm left with nothing but a target on my head. Is that the way it works?'

'How much do you trust your girlfriend?' I say. 'She could have handed you over by now, she knew where you were. She could have dumped you in it, but she wants you. Do you want her?'

I see him squirm. I realize that despite the fact he's got a death sentence over his head, his real issue is whether or not to be with his wife, or to be with his fancy woman. Circumstances are calling him out, asking him to make a run abroad with one or ditch her and stay with the other, facing the consequences. I'm really not that sure how this works, but I know where to lean.

'You want your freedom, is that it?' I say 'Well, I'll get you it. You give me the money; I'll get you out of this and you'll live scot-free. And you will continue to play these two women off on each other. That's what you want, isn't it? Just to go back to how things were. Well, I'll get rid of Sergei, I'll sort up the loose ends, but I need the money. You don't give me the money, I'll contact Sergei, hand you over and he can extract the money from you. It's up to him what happens to you. I doubt Laura will be able to stop him and you'll probably be dead within an hour. Probably not a nice death either. I saw the head inside the plastic bag. I reckon they chopped up each bit, one at a time.'

I see him squirm. He tries to look away from me, but then looks back, trying to gauge how accurate I am. And that's the thing, I'm not lying. If I hand him over, and I take Susan, we'll be in difficulties because they'll come after us. But we'll last a hell of a lot longer than he will. One of the problems with running is getting all the paperwork together, but I do know one thing, my little boat is somewhere for us to go and hide. We can then steal a ride, stay out, go for the quieter places. I could probably even see my way off to Europe, get a plane from there to America or South America, Australia, New Zealand, wherever. I could take this little family that I've got into trouble and go somewhere.

Actually, sounds quite nice, especially if Maggie was with me. But I'm also not willing to take defeat. Sergei is a man that's using people. He's taken a business that's been decent and turned it, albeit with the consent of the owners, into something that exploits people. Exploits people in a far-off country, exploits trafficked people here, and exploits the good teenagers buying the goods. I've pretty much made up my mind. He needs to be shut down and I will have my way. I just hand in the evidence. And then the good police force of the day does it. But Susan's screwed that up.

'So, what's it to be? I've got to phone him in a minute. Tell Sergei where we're meeting. What's he getting? You and the money? Or just the money? Correction—or just you?'

If his hands weren't tied together along with his feet, he'd be shaking like anything. I'm not sure if he'd be able to stand. He may even have soiled himself for all I know. But he's out of options. He doesn't trust Laura. He probably doesn't trust me that much, but he hasn't got another option.

'Glenview farm,' he says. 'Go behind the storage for hay. The biggest barn they've got. Walk behind it, twenty paces, copse of trees and dig there. That's where it will be.'

'Where's Glenview farm?' I say. 'I take it's on this side of Loch Ryan.' He nods, 'You're only about half an hour away. It's right down, close to the tip. You can look out into the Irish sea. It's not a bad viewpoint once you get past the farm.'

I leave the caravan and grab hold of Maggie, telling her to stay inside and keep an eye on our guest, telling her Kirsten will come with me. She gives me an angry look when I tell her to get in the car, as we drive off to find Glenview farm. I try to engage with her, but she's pissed at me and that's fine, but it was her sister that got us into this position, not me. And I need her on our game tomorrow because we're going to need help.

I drive along the coast road down towards Glenview farm. All of a sudden, I see the location I need. It's an abandoned building, a small carpet factory, or at least that's what it used to be, apparently. There's still a lot of waste about, old signs that are gradually falling down, but I drive in across the concrete. Making my way inside the large building, I see some offices on one side, broken windows, a lot of glass on the site. You can see the evidence of rats running around, as well. It's good for a handover. There's one way in and there's one way out. If we do it inside, that suits me.

'This is where we'll get your sister back tomorrow,' I say to Kirsten but she just shrugs. 'It won't be pretty. I'll need your help. You're going to lay some traps down once everybody arrives. So, I need you to listen because in the next half hour, you're going to pick up and understand everything you need to do.' Again, she shrugs her shoulders. 'Look,' I say, 'I don't care if you hate me, but if you want your sister back tomorrow, you'll listen up good.'

Half an hour later, we're heading out, descending down to Glenview farm. I can see the tractors moving back and forward and we have to park along the road a little way. Getting out, we move across a field and I see the large barn he's talking about. I run to the back of it, count my steps out, and spy the copse of trees. I got a small spade in my hand, one that fits in cars. It's collapsible and light but it will be adequate for what I need. Kirsten sits down on her bum watching me dig. She's never seen somebody dig with one hand and it's not easy. You use your feet a lot. You need to have a good rest and it's slow going, but she never offers to help. I guess it's my fault. I'm paying for my mistakes.

I get the impression from Russell Hadleigh, that while he likes to engage in things, sometimes risky things, he's not good at following things through, finishing them off. Maybe that's why he's made such an arse of the relationship between his wife and Laura, but he's certainly made an arse of burying this thing. It's only four foot down and I find the suitcase. Lifting it out, I don't look at it and suddenly shovel all the dirt back again, stamping down over where it was buried, replacing some branches and leaves he had over the top. Kirsten scowls again, as I pick up the case and indicate we should go.

Getting back to the car, both the case and the spade go in the boot and I drive off to the tip of the land. It's a real vantage point so I pull up the car. I might as well have something nice to look at when I'm getting into the fight of my life. I'm amazed how little money this is all about. That's the thing about money, people get hyped up over the smallest amounts sometimes. Kirsten sits beside me on the bench. As I lift the case up onto my lap, I tell her to flick open the latches, which she dutifully does, and our eyes light up.

I don't generally tend to see a lot of hundred-pound notes. And at the moment I'm looking at an awful lot of them. I take one stack, hand it to Kirsten and ask her to count them. She does so, and then puts it back. I then count up the rows, nine across. And then ask how much is in there. I see her do the math.

'Bloody hell, Paddy,' she says, 'There's got to be a million.' I'm sure my knees are shaking slightly because I've never held this sort of cash. If it weren't for Susan being held, the temptation to just grab it and run would probably be too strong for me, but I need to do what's right with it. As I close it back over, Kirsten says to me, "Why don't we keep some of it? Give him most of it and keep some of it? If he's going to come after us, we're going to need money to get away."

I shake my head. "If you know anything, they keep coming. If the money's missing, they'll get their money back. They'll know who's got it. If things go right, Kirsten, we are not running." She looks at me in disbelief and I don't blame her. For a moment, I sit, looking out to sea, breathing in the fresh air, watching the clouds roll in. I can see the shower before me. The drizzle earlier on in the day has now dissipated, shafts of sunlight breaking through before another shower will hit. I perch there for half an hour, thoughts going around my head while Kirsten sits in silence with me. Then I take her back to the car and drive her to the caravan.

We put the case full of money at the front of the caravan, stuck under one of the sofa seats, which lifts up to reveal a large storage space underneath. I'm not sure it's ever held something like this, probably just a place for plastic cups, drinks, crockery, and whatever else people keep on holiday. But for tonight, it's going to make this caravan worth over a hundred times its value.

Outside, Maggie comes to me, puts her hands on my shoulders, and asks if everything is okay for tomorrow. I nod.

'But I need to go and get something, something in case everything goes wrong.' She looks at me and then I think she understands. 'Can you handle a weapon?' I ask and she nods. 'Then I'll get one for you. Kirsten?'

'Don't offer her one. You hold a gun, they're more likely to kill you, more likely to shoot you first. She doesn't have one, she might have time to run.'

It's a rather bleak assessment of our chances tomorrow, but she may be right. I simply nod at Maggie before walking off to the car.

The drive into Stranraer and out the other side to the Marina, where Craigantlet is moored, takes less than an hour. I pick up some paperwork, walk around the boat with the man who's been cleaning it up and eventually nod, shake hands, and thank him profusely. Once inside, I take it away from the maintenance slip, and moor it up for the night. Climbing inside, I go straight to my bunk and reach into a compartment that I haven't opened in two years.

Inside are two handguns and enough ammunition to take on a squad of men. I take out a plastic bag, place the guns in it, and the ammunition and tie up the top of it. When I leave my beloved boat, I tap it gently, telling her to be ready for our return, just in case things don't go well tomorrow. She's always got enough tea and provisions to keep us going. It won't be Cordon Bleu, but it'll be enough.

I sail here enough to know the places to hide. One bright side of this whole escapade is that no one knows I have a boat, but they may eventually track it though because I've used my proper name. Let's hope it doesn't come to that. I drive back across town, picking up a couple of pizzas on the way, along with a bottle of whiskey. There's going to be a lot of fear in the caravan and we all need a good night's sleep.

On arrival, everyone's inside, and we share all the pizzas, feeding our guest. He sits up on the bed, hungrily devouring what's in front of him. I thought about undoing his hands, maybe putting them on a piece of string, tied to somewhere, but frankly he's been a pain in the arse and he's also exploited a lot of people. While I might be able to get him out of this alive and free, I sure as hell am not enjoying it.

I spend the evening sitting at the front of the caravan, playing snakes and ladders with Maggie and Kirsten. It's the only game available. You'd think they could stock it a bit better for tourists. The whiskey disappears. Once Kirsten has gone off to bed, I take out the plastic bag from earlier, place it on the table and open it and hand the gun to Maggie, asking if she knows how to handle it. She drops out the chamber, places the bullets inside, pops it in again and I watch her click off the safety. I look at her giving that glance that asks the question, how the hell she knows how to do that, but she's ahead of me.

'When I lived with him, we weren't always in the greatest places when he travelled with the army. And he taught me, taught me how to handle a firearm in case I ever needed it. It's not something you forget. Especially after the date at the firing range. Let's hope I don't need it.'

'You ever shot someone?'

Her face goes sullen, her eyes seemingly in pain. 'God knows it was only an intruder, but he was after me, not any of my possessions. But you don't forget it,' she says.

'No, you don't.' I take my gun, and load it up, thinking back to the last time I used one of these in anger. The things you saw in the force back then, you don't want brought up.

Chapter 22

There's a knot deep in my stomach as we arrive at the warehouse I'd scouted before. Maggie's in the front seat with me, Kirsten in the back, and our package is in the boot. Of course, Hadleigh wasn't happy about that, but he is the package, so he stays out of sight. You don't want to arrive at a place, people see him in the car, and somebody jump in and grab him. Better they're not sure where he is.

We park up, and I keep everyone in the car, telling Maggie to sit behind the driver's seat while I check out what's going on. She's under specific instructions to leave if things get too hot, not to wait for me. Better she has at least one daughter than none at all.

Once I know the building's clear, I return to the car and Kirsten gets out, disappearing off with something from our boot. Now we take the judge out of the back and sit him in the rear seats. You can see the tension on his face. I haven't told him exactly what I'm going to do—that would be too much of a giveaway. He needs to look panicked, needs to look shocked.

I hear a car turn up. When I look over, I see the deep red car of Laura Sutherland, her brunette hair waving in the wind as she steps out. It's the broken windows in the building allowing the fresh breeze from outside. Because we're out of the sunshine, there's a bit of a chill on our skin. Like there wasn't one already.

She parks away from us and stands in front of her car, looking over at me. She's got no one with her. Her protective bouncer, the one she put out in front of her Judge, is no longer here and I wonder if that's at Sergei's request. To show up with force would mean she doesn't trust him.

My weapon sits on my right hip, incredibly obvious and that's the point. I didn't bring it to use it. I brought it to make sure someone doesn't use one on me. Maggie's is concealed, tucked inside her jacket. I don't want her to draw it unless she is in trouble, in case they see her as a target to take down first. There are too many variables, too many people that can get hurt now, and that's why the knot in my stomach keeps getting deeper.

I can hear a car outside, and it rolls in through the large empty doors at the far end, the same ones we've all driven through already. It's a black van and when it pulls up, two large and rough-looking men step out of it and stand either side of the van.

Another man gets out, walks around scanning the place before stepping back inside the van, saying something in Russian to someone. Then Sergei comes out. Just Sergei. He walks over to Laura for some reason, gives her a kiss on the cheek and then takes her by the hand, bringing her firmly towards his own vehicle. He's worried she'll cut and run, so he's keeping everyone close together.

I step forward into the middle ground between us, and Sergei does the same, his goons remaining at the vehicle. I can't see Sergei's weapon, but I'm sure he has one somewhere. As we draw close, I realize this bald-headed man is not as tall as me.

It's strange how the small ones always seem to end up leading, like they've got some sort of chip on their shoulder. Maybe that's it. Maybe it's something else.

He's dressed in black trousers, a black jacket on top and looks like a stereotypical thug, but he's cleverer than that. After all, he's running the operation here. We stop about six feet apart and he's got a smile on his face.

'We meet again,' he says. 'Quite the golfer, and now the poker player. How long have you been investigating me?' he says.

'Who says I'm investigating you?'

'Your friend talks, Mr Smythe.'

'So, she's still alive? I'd like to see that.' Sergei nods, turns around to his goons and gives a motion with his hand. The side of the van is opened and the figure of Susan, her hair a bit of a mess, but otherwise looking in reasonably good condition, steps out.

Sergei turns back to me, as I hear a gasp from Maggie behind me. 'You bring the mother with you?' he says. 'A bit of a risk. You don't seem to have too many professional buddies.'

'I don't need professional buddies, but I do have some and yes, we have been investigating you, and we have the footage and everything else, all ready to go if I don't walk away from here. All ready to go if she doesn't walk away.' I nod my head towards Susan. 'All ready to go, if anyone that comes with me, doesn't walk away.'

'And if I take my money and my man and drive out?' says Sergei.

'Well then that's the last we see of each other and I'll send you what I've got, and you can destroy it.'

'But how do I know you won't have more than that?'

'You don't,' I say with a wry smile. 'You'll have to trust me on that. But then again, once I've played my hand, you're exposed, your boss is exposed, and I'm exposed again. You'd be free to come after me. Whilst we have it, we keep that uneasy tension, just like the cold war all over again, Sergei.'

'Let me see your side of the bargain.'

I turn around and walk back to the car. Stepping to the rear door, I open it and pull out Russell Hadleigh. He's handcuffed and I let him walk forward with me. Behind me, Maggie's pulling out the briefcase with all of the money. When I glance round at her, I see she's nervous, but she's just about holding it together. Her eyes are less on the case, and more on her daughter. When I get up to Sergei, I look beyond him. 'Are you bringing her forward as well?'

Sergei turns around and walks slowly back and he's full of confidence. There's no air of tension in him, but there's tension in me. The cold air round my neck gives a lie as to why I've got goose bumps. It's the tension seeing Susan. Sergei now brings her forward, a goon on his side. As she gets closer, I can see her face is bruised. They've roughed her up certainly and that's probably why she talked. She needed to talk because if she hadn't, they'd have roughed her up a hell of a lot more.

Sergei stops this time, some twelve feet apart and has a strong hand on Susan's arm. She's quite tearful and she blurts out a 'Sorry, Paddy.' But I hold up my hand indicating she should stay quiet. I don't need her emotion in the middle of this, there's too much to watch. My eyes scan from the goon to Sergei, to the two at the back standing beside the vehicle like some sentry at the gates.

'Shall we do this?' I say, and I push Russell Hadleigh forward a step. He's resistant, so I draw my weapon slowly, placing it in his back, 'Walk forward, two steps,' I say, trying to make sure my voice doesn't show any emotion. Like I've done this a thousand times before. I haven't. That's the problem. Despite all of my experience in these sorts of things, I certainly haven't done this before.

Sergei pushes Susan forward and she half stumbles before standing up. They haven't cuffed her, they haven't tied her up at all, so they must have given her a beating to keep her in place.

Hadleigh walks forward. I say, 'Susan, every step he takes, you take one towards me, and pass in the middle.' Slowly they cross, Susan looking up at him only briefly, and I see Russell Hadleigh begin to shake as he arrives at his new captors. Sergei's staring at him, his face right in the taller man's.

'Don't worry, my dear Judge,' says Sergei, 'what she received is nothing to what you will. Mr Porterfield, he learned the error of his ways.'

'And where is Mr Porterfield,' I say, 'now that he's been moved?' Sergei casts a glance at me, and I see the first sign of nervousness. He obviously didn't realize just how much I knew. Maybe he didn't know to ask, and that's why Susan didn't tell him. 'I mean, where is all of Andrew Porterfield? Every bit.'

'Don't worry, Mr Smythe,' says Sergei, 'it's been taken care of. The ashes have been scattered. He's just another missing man, another sad accident, another boat come down on the water. If you holiday in the right country, it's easy to make these things happen.' And with that Sergei waves to Laura, calling her over to him. She throws her hair back and tries to stride forward confidently, but I can see the quiver, the nervous shake as she approaches. 'You leave your car here,' says Sergei. 'I need you to come with us and dispose of this man.' Laura looks at him in horror but then she nods her head and spits out the words, 'Of course. You want me to clean up my own mess.'

And now it's Russell's turn to start to shake violently. He begins to shout at Laura, and I watch as his trousers become stained around the crotch area. A man suddenly realizing he's going to his death, a death by the hand of his lover. It must destroy him; after all, she has been protecting him so far. No wonder he's panicked, his bladder finally collapsing.

'And if you will, Mr Smythe, my money.' I nod, turn to Susan who's still standing beside me. 'Walk to the car.'

I get another, 'I'm sorry, Paddy.'

I give her a harsh 'Shush!' and tell her to get in the car. Looking over my other shoulder, I call Maggie forward and I watch as her face looks at her daughter, a sense of relief sweeping over it. And yet I can tell, she knows we're not clear yet. Maggie steps up beside me and I tell her to hand the money over to Sergei. She takes some six steps forward, leaves it down at his feet, and walks back to stand beside me. And there's something in Sergei's face, something that chills me to the core. I can see he isn't happy with the plan so far. Something is wrong.

'Let's tie this up a bit more,' says Sergei, 'make sure we're all in the circle. Make sure no one speaks.' He reaches forward and pulls Russell Hadleigh down onto his knees, the tall man now beneath his captor. Sergei reaches inside his jacket, and I see him pull out a gun.

'Whoa,' I say, 'easy,' as I raise my own weapon. 'What are you doing?' He turns and smiles at me. His fingers around his weapon, letting it dangle. 'Do not panic, Mr Smythe. If I wanted to kill you, we would have done it by now. No, Miss Sutherland is going to tidy up our mess. Would you be so kind, Laura?' he says. He hands the weapon to her and she can barely hold it. The once proud woman is starting to cry and the bearing, the upright back, the shoulders looking so confident are gone, and she's hunched like a wreck. She's standing ten feet away and then pulls her gun, pointing it at Russell Hadleigh, the gun shaking. And I tell Maggie to look away.

'There's no need, Sergei. There's no need.'

'What did you think I was going to do with him, Mr Smythe? You know fine rightly, once I drive out of here, he's dead. We kill him now, then you're in the mix as well. You'll have concealed it, knowing all about it. But if you go to the police straight away, we will come after you. I'm just tying the knot tighter.'

My mind's racing. How do we get out of this one? If she shoots, she shoots, and we have to keep our uneasy silence. There's a hush, with only the occasional rustle of the trees outside, the breeze still stiff.

'Go on, Miss Sutherland. Go on, or our deal's off. And if our deal's off and then we won't be here, and neither will you.'

With that, Laura looks up into Sergei's eyes. She's raging. She's wild but her lower hand still holds the gun pointed at Russell Hadleigh on his knees. I can see a storm inside her. She's not the obedient, injured party now; she's angry at being manipulated, of being played. This is a woman that's used to being in control, and it's been stripped away from her. She's looking at being the minor player in this business, and also at having blood in her hands, killing a man that to all intents and purposes she loves, in whatever way that works for them. I see the gun swing away from Russell Hadleigh, but I'm not the only one that sees that. The next few moments happen so quick.

There are two loud cracks of gunfire. One is Laura shooting at Sergei, and I can see him reel after it, clutching towards his stomach. The other gunfire comes from Sergei himself, managing to pull out a weapon by the time she's fired. It's a snapshot from him and it catches Laura's shoulder, spinning her around. The two things happen almost together, and I see her drop her weapon, stumbling off towards her car.

Sergei hits the deck, his weapon falling away, but his goons start to run forward. Russell Hadleigh's in tears. One of those things when people think they've been shot when they haven't. He was expecting it, and his body's probably in shock from wondering what's not happened to him. Sergei's goons step forward and I have only a moment to react. As I watch Laura stumble towards her car, I draw my weapon, pointing it at Sergei's head.

His goons reach for theirs, but I hear a cry from behind me, telling them to stop. It's Maggie and I'm sure she has a weapon in front of her.

'Easy, everyone,' I shout loudly. 'Easy! Driver, step out of the van. Out of the van now, or I'll kill him.' Sergei's moaning in pain. He's been shot in the belly and it looks like it's bleeding bad. It's not what I was expecting. I thought we were going to have to stop the vehicle on the way out, to extract Russell Hadleigh, but this is an opportunity. 'Guns on the ground,' I say. 'All of you, guns on the ground, or your boss gets it.'

The goons drop their weapons. I see the man in the van standing beside it, gingerly taking his weapon from inside his jacket and leaving it on the ground too. 'Your boss needs help,' I say, 'and this is what's going to happen. You're going to come forward, pick him up and take him into the van. You'll get your weapons back, but in pieces inside the van. You'll get the money and you'll drive off, and then we will disappear, and you won't bother us again. You'll forget the name, Paddy Smythe. You'll forget the good ladies with me. And you can take up your relationship with this Judge and Miss Sutherland at your convenience. And you'll never hear from me again unless anyone in my party sees you. At which point we release everything, and your operation will be brought down, and your boss will not be best pleased. But if you keep your terms, you'll never see us either. Am I understood?'

Sergei looks up at me. 'It's bad,' I say. 'I know it's bad and you need help, but am I understood? Because if I don't get an answer, I'll let you bleed out right in front of me. Understand this, I'm perfectly capable of disposing of you all right now.' There's a harshness in my voice, a tone that says I've done this before, and I know I'm getting through to Sergei. He's beginning to panic a little because he knows his time's short if he doesn't move.

'I will not come near you,' he says. 'You have my word, for that's all we have in this business. You are free to go.' With that, I take the gun away from his head and tell his goons to walk forward. I'm not totally daft. Maggie's still got her weapon trained on him; their guns are on the ground. They pick up Sergei and take him into the back of the van, Maggie following him the whole way. I take their weapons, empty them with a slight of hand anyone would be proud of, before throwing them inside the vehicle. Once we've packed the money inside, the large sliding door of the vehicle's shut and they drive off.

With Maggie stood at the door, her gun still at the ready, I collect Kirsten from the shadows. She had a spike trap ready, ready to blow the tires of the vehicle so we could rescue Russell

Hadleigh if I decided to. But Laura Sutherland threw a spanner in the works, and I think it's a spanner that's worked if we play this right, but we need to get to ground.

I check Laura Sutherland's wound. It's fairly minor as she was hit across the shoulder and it's not bleeding bad. It's certainly patchable, nothing that should require a visit to anywhere, if she treats it right. I uncuff Russell Hadleigh and tell him to go with Laura. He looks at me as if I'm insane. After all, the woman was pointing a gun at his head. But I point out she didn't shoot him—she shot Sergei, so he's probably all right.

I give them strict instructions to go to ground and not to be seen and they disappear off in the red car, Russell still smelling of urine. The disgusting, sharp smell that fresh urine gives off, grabbing your nose, making you want to turn your head away. I don't want to know where they go, but they've been told to just go to ground until I contact them. I have Laura's number and she has a large bodyguard who will no doubt make sure they stay safe. Maybe they'll even head back to that small house.

And then after a quick tidy up of the scene, I'm back sitting in the car. Kirsten in the front beside me now because Maggie's in the rear holding her daughter in her arms, both crying.

'Thank you, Paddy,' says Kirsten, and yet I feel it's a little begrudging. I wonder what I've done to deserve the thanks; after all, I brought her sister into this. I've dragged their whole family with me, getting them out of the mess that I brought them into.

'And now we go to ground,' I say, 'because this isn't over yet. I hope Martha knows what she's doing.'

Chapter 23

The next few hours are busy. I don't trust Russell Hadleigh not to give up to Laura where the caravan was, and then somehow get it back under some sort of bargain to Sergei. So, we don't go back there. Instead, I drive right into the Marina and then drop Maggie and her two daughters on board Craigantlet. I park the car up, return, sail Craigantlet just a little down the coast and anchor, a little off the shore.

Craigantlet is a part of my life I keep incredibly quiet. That's my hidey-hole, my place away from everyone. And if I want to disappear, that's where I'll usually be. It's a bit of a squash with four people on board, but that's all right, because I get back off quickly. Taking my little dingy back to shore, I hide it up, grab a taxi and get back in the car. I now change hire cars, this time hiring one under a different identity I've got.

I call a travel firm and get a last-minute booking on a coach tour to the north of Scotland, making the booking in Alison Hadleigh's name. She was surprised to receive a call from me and it takes a bit of convincing, but within an hour, she's in a taxi for Glasgow and within another three, she'll be on her way out of the large city and heading for the Highlands. It's a three-day tour. I'm sure after that I'll know what's what.

Sitting in the car by the sea thinking things over, I've already sent a text to Martha to go ahead with the next phase once she sees the money.

I take a spin by the quaint house that Russell Hadleigh was being hidden in by Laura. And sure enough, that's where they are. I looked as much for me to tag my own cards, make sure I know what's going on. On the pavement I see the same large goon outside walking up and down, making sure no one bothers them.

Looking at the sea, I realize it's time to be patient, time to let other people take the weight. I do a scan around the different houses, past Maggie's, Alison Hadleigh's and Laura Sutherland's, but I can't see anyone watching them. It's later on in the day when my phone rings and I see Martha's image on it. She's not using a private number, not keeping us off the record, so she'll be talking in code.

'How are you, buddy?' she says. 'I take it that the holidays are not too troubling.'

'No,' I say. 'At the moment, the water is very calm up here. I don't think it's been disturbed by anyone. Just the way we like it.'

'I wish I could say that for me,' she says. 'The water's churning like anything. Got very rough. One of the swimmers I thought was going to be lost. In fact, still could be lost.'

'Did he build his sandcastle?' I ask, referring in code to the money. 'Did he build it in the right place?'

'He put it in one place, but someone moved it,' she says. 'And his dad wasn't happy about that. It seems there was already a lot of heat on. I don't think the family was that happy to begin with.'

'You always have the best holidays,' I tell her. And I think to myself, well done, Martha.

I spend the next few days on and off Craigantlet with Maggie and her family. Susan's struggling to look me in the eye despite the fact that I've told her a thousand times, it's fine. Maggie thanks me, but really, she did well herself. And I think Kirsten's lightened up to me a little bit more. But after three days, the boredom starts to set in and they're desperate to get back to shore. I get to walk on the land every day, checking the places, making sure the houses aren't being broken into or checked over, and making sure Russell and Laura are still okay. Just as much to make sure they don't do anything dumb.

I get a text after four days from Martha. It's on the secure line and there's not many words. Simply, Russians pulling out, local man disappeared, scratched off the employment list. And that would appear to be that for the Russian involvement. They've cut and run.

I leave it another day before bringing everyone back off the boat and witness their joy at getting back to their house. The girls are all smiles when they hear the Russian involvement is over, but I see Maggie being a little bit more circumspect and she takes me aside.

'So, he's dead. They killed him. I guess it was him or us?'

'Ultimately, yes,' I say. 'Not what I would have done and not the way I wanted it to finish. But Susan's alive. I'm alive. We all walk away except for Sergei and maybe his goons, but he was scum of the earth,' I say.

'All God's children,' she says, bringing up the words my mother used to say. I had convinced myself that the guy was as good dead as he was alive, and she throws that in. But I'll live with it. All in all, it's about as good a result as I could have got.

The next day, I'm at Alison Hadleigh's and see the taxi driver drop her off. When she opens her front door and we step into the living room, I shake her hand.

'Thanks for going away. I needed to make sure that you were safe, and you are. No one's coming after you, no one's linked it to you, but the next few days are going to be rough. And you're going to have to make a decision.'

'A decision? What do you mean?' she asks. 'Am I'm safe. What's going on?'

Her confusion is understandable because I kept her in the dark on just about everything, but I'm not going to let these things just lie. I have her take her stuff inside, get changed and then I take her to the beach as the day turns toward the afternoon, sat on a rock away from everyone.

'You don't know what I've been doing,' I tell her. 'I saw your life and what you get up to.' This doesn't shock her; in fact, she tells me that I should have joined her. But what does shock her is when I tell her what her husband's been up to with regards to his business. At one point, I see tears in her eyes as she realizes he was nearly killed.

But then I tell her point blank about who has been looking after him and how he's probably renewed his affair, if not a lot more, with Laura Sutherland. I remember the two women at the hotel and the way they looked at each other and I'd seen hatred right there.

'That bitch,' she says. 'He always wanted her; she could control him like putty. He wouldn't have wanted to be involved in that nonsense, having spent his whole life as a judge, but she had told him—she'd have pushed for the money. That's all she wants. To dominate. To be at the top.'

'And you don't?' I say, a little incredulously. 'I saw you vying with her at that so-called party. You want to be top as well.'

'I merely play,' she says. 'And I have a lot of fun when I play, but I can play whatever role you want. But not her. She wants it all.' I decide to leave this convoluted way of thinking and get back to practicalities telling her we're going to go to meet the pair of them. Depending on his reaction, I'll see what my next move is.

As we drive along back to the house where Russell and Laura have been hiding, I wonder how it will go. Who will he stay with? We pull up into the small drive and almost instantly, there's the large goon. I step out with my arm in the air, telling him to be calm.

'What's going on?' he asks.

'Sergei's gone. That side of it's over.' Then I nod towards Alison. 'That is Judge Hadleigh's wife,' I say. 'This might be one for you and me to stay out of.' The man looks at me, and then nods, but follows us into the house. There's a stunned silence when we go into the room and within a couple of minutes, the accusations are flying. I interrupt briefly to tell them that I'll be outside with my large friend.

It's two hours later and we're sitting on the bottom of my car, the large man enjoying a cigarette, talking over times and how things have got rough. I tell him he's got a good punch and we laugh a bit about my sneaking in and him catching me. He's not a nasty man, a proper protection agent, someone who is there for his clients and I understand him fully. And if I'm honest, as far as this day goes, it's the most enjoyable two hours chewing the fat with someone from the business.

And then our mutual camaraderie is broken up as Alison emerges from the building, shortly followed by her husband, Laura clinging on to him. 'Take me home,' says Alison.

'And what about him?' I say.

'That little shit is staying with the hussy.'

'Okay,' I say. 'Don't get in the car yet. You'll want to hear this.' I make my way over to Laura and Russell and I explain to them that the footage I have showing where all the clothing came from and how the business was running, is getting released to the police.

'I'm sure you can explain your way out of it. That you didn't understand, and you weren't there. Laura is not in the footage, but it will bring the business down.'

I also explain my fee will not be paid by Alison. It will be coming from them and it will be in a bank account that I specify within the next twenty-four hours. And beyond that, I don't want to see or hear them again because if they cause me any trouble, Laura's part in all of this will get brought up. I'm sure an arrest will follow.

With that, they storm inside, but I know my points are made. As I depart, the large bodyguard taps me on the shoulder and extends a hand. 'Well played, sir,' he says. 'I've never seen her so lost for words. Well played.' I wish him all the best and step inside the car to drive Alison Hadleigh home.

Once back at the house, there's tears, there's anger, there's several swift drinks and then there's a thank you to me. One request, do I want to stay? I shake my head explaining she's my client, or at least was, and I make a rule not to get involved with them. It's a bit of a bitter let down that I'm not even vaguely interested. She asks me to stay until a friend arrives, to which I agree as she's a little shaken about Russell's betrayal. I know it may seem strange given the lifestyle she leads but I think I begin to understand her. This pantomime is just sex to her, and these are really games she plays. She never thought he'd actually go with someone for real.

John Carson arrives, spreading delight over Alison's face as he walks up the drive. Oh well, things might be all right after all, although I do recall he's married. I try not to work out how these things will play out. It's their lives now and I want to get back to mine.

It's evening when I get to Maggie's, nine o'clock and the little family are waiting for me when I get back. I tell them simply that's it—it's all closed down. There might be some eruptions at the golf club when it's found out that the judge has left his wife but other than that, hopefully things will go back to normal. Although there'll be no clothing, no fairly traded brand for a lot of the teenagers in the area. Still they'll move on.

Susan tries to apologize to me again, and I stop her, telling her to go to bed because my partner needs a good sleep before she starts work in the morning. She grins before disappearing up the stairs, Kirsten following her. I'm left with Maggie in the front room.

'So, you really are taking her on?' she says.

'Yes,' I say. 'I've been thinking about some of the stuff you've said over the last few days. Maybe I need to go a little bit more legit, get some basic cases. A little bit less stuff on the dark side. Having an office will do that, help me get some normal investigations. And we'll keep her busy. She is keen, determined, just a little green.'

'So, you're sticking around?' says Maggie. And for the first time I detect a little wobble in her voice.

'Of course,' I say, and allow myself the luxury of taking in the view of this woman that seems to be grabbing at me.

'You can stay over if you want,' she says. 'God knows you

deserves it.' She takes my hand and I know she wants to lead me upstairs, although I detect hesitation in her. She's not wholly comfortable, and I think this is maybe her ploy to make sure I stay, but she doesn't need to. I hold my ground, but she tries to walk off and I pull her back.

'I'm going to do this properly,' I say. She looks at me, her eyes wondering, trying to seek out what's in my mind. A dangerous place for any woman to go, a man's mind, but this time she'll be pleasantly surprised. 'Do you like horror movies?' I ask.

'No,' she says. 'Can't stand them.'

'That's a pity,' I say. 'Because there's a new one at the cinema tonight, late show, eleven o'clock. I thought you might want to go on a date.'

She grins. 'Only because you're going,' she says. 'I'll get my coat.'

We sit in the small cinema and I can count maybe six people in the place. The film, if I'm honest, is crap and I'm not sure Maggie's even watching it. But what I do know is I've got my arm around her and her head's on my shoulder and this is a rather good result.

Turn over to discover the new Patrick Smythe series!

TURN OVER TO DISCOVER THE NEW PATRICK SMYTHE SERIES!

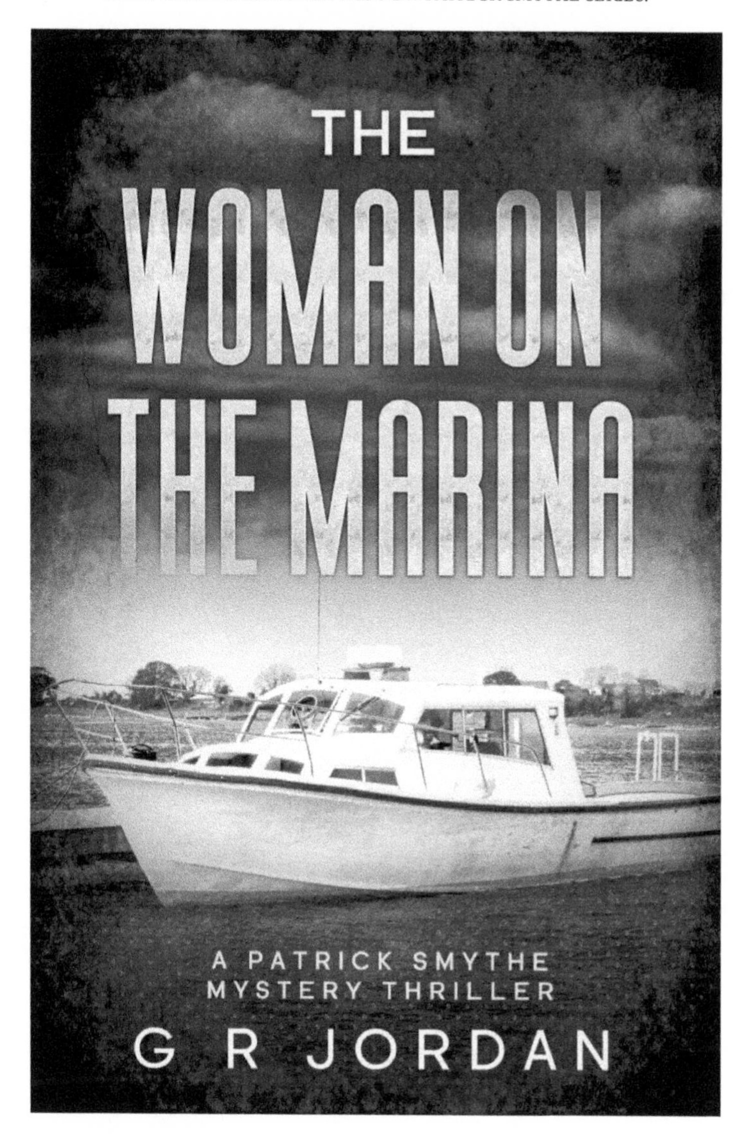

Start your Patrick Smythe journey here!

Patrick Smythe is a former Northern Irish policeman who

after suffering an amputation after a bomb blast, takes to the sea between the west coast of Scotland and his homeland to ply his trade as a private investigator. Join Paddy as he tries to work to his own ethics while knowing how to bend the rules he once enforced. Working from his beloved motorboat 'Craigantlet', Paddy decides to rescue a drug mule in this short story from the pen of G R Jordan.

Join G R Jordan's monthly newsletter about forthcoming releases and special writings for his tribe of avid readers and then receive your free Patrick Smythe short story.

Go to *https://bit.ly/PatrickSmythe* for your Patrick Smythe journey to start!

About the Author

GR Jordan is a self-published author who finally decided at forty that in order to have an enjoyable lifestyle, his creative beast within would have to be unleashed. His books mirror that conflict in life where acts of decency contend with self-promotion, goodness stares in horror at evil, and kindness blindsides us when we at our worst. Corrupting our world with his parade of wondrous and horrific characters, he highlights everyday tensions with fresh eyes whilst taking his methodical, intelligent mainstays on a roller-coaster ride of dilemmas, all the while suffering the banter of their provocative sidekicks.

A graduate of Loughborough University where he masqueraded as a chemical engineer but ultimately played American football, Gary had worked at changing the shape of cereal flakes and pulled a pallet truck for a living. Watching vegetables freeze at -40'C was another career highlight and he was also one of the Scottish Highlands "blind" air traffic controllers.

These days he has graduated to answering a telephone to people in trouble before telephoning other people to sort it out.

Having flirted with most places in the UK, he is now based in the Isle of Lewis in Scotland where his free time is spent between raising a young family with his wife, writing, figuring out how to work a loom and caring for a small flock of chickens. Luckily, his writing is influenced by his varied work and life experience as the chickens have not been the poetical inspiration he had hoped for!

You can connect with me on:

- https://grjordan.com
- https://twitter.com/carpetless
- https://facebook.com/carpetlessleprechaun

Subscribe to my newsletter:

- https://bit.ly/PatrickSmythe

Also by G R Jordan

G R Jordan writes across multiple genres including crime, dark and action adventure fantasy, feel good fantasy, mystery thriller and horror fantasy. Below is a selection of his work grouped together in their genres. Whilst all books are available across online stores, signed copies are available at his personal shop

The Graves of Calgary Bay: A Patrick Smythe Mystery Thriller

https://grjordan.com/product/the-graves-at-calgary-bay

A naked body found on a lonely island. A band of sailors lifting graves in the dead of night. Can Paddy discover the secret that led a sheltered young man to a most gruesome death?

In his second full novel, former one-armed policeman Patrick Smythe takes to the Isle of Mull at the request of a distraught mother, looking for the truth of why her only son was found dead on the small island of Gometra. Along with his new feisty assistant, Susan Calderwood, Paddy uncovers the true story of a brutal death and incurs the wrath of local smugglers, sailors and a well-known photographer. But when things turn nasty, can Paddy plot a way out and see that justice is done?

Those who mess with the dead bring a reckoning onto themselves!

Water's Edge: A Highlands and Islands Detective Thriller (Highlands & Islands Detective Book 1)
https://grjordan.com/product/waters-edge
A body discovered by the rocks. A broken detective returns to a scene of past tragedy. Will the pain of the past prevent him from seeing the present?

Detective Inspector Macleod returns to his island home twenty years after the painful loss of his wife. With a disposition forged in strong religious conservatism, he must bond with his new partner, the free spirited and upcoming female star of the force, to seek the killer of a young woman and shine a light on the evil beneath the surface. To do so, he must once again stand in the place where he lost everything. Only at the water's edge, will everything be made new.

The rising tide brings all things to the surface.

The Bothy: A Highlands and Islands Detective Thriller (Highlands & Islands Detective Book 2)
https://grjordan.com/product/the-bothy
Two bodies in a burnt out love nest. A cultish lifestyle and children moulded by domination. Can Macleod unravel the Black Isle mystery before the killer dispenses judgement again?

DI Macleod heads for the Black Isle as winter sets in to unravel the mystery of two lovers in a burned out bothy. With his feisty partner DC McGrath, he must unravel the connection between a family living under a cultish cloud and a radio station whose staff are being permanently retired. In the dark of winter, can Macleod shine a light on the shadowy relationships driving a killer to their murderous tasks?

Forgetting your boundaries has never been so deadly!

The Horror Weekend (Highlands & Islands Detective Book 3)
https://grjordan.com/product/the-horror-weekend

A last-minute replacement on a role-playing weekend. One fatal accident after another. Can Macleod overcome the snowstorm from hell to stop a killer before the guest list becomes obsolete?

Detectives Macleod and McGrath join a bizarre cast of characters at a remote country estate on the Isle of Harris where fantasy and horror are the order of the day. But when regular accidents happen, Macleod sees a killer at work and needs to uncover what links the dead. Hampered by a snowstorm that has closed off the outside world, he must rely on Hope McGrath before they become one of the victims.
It's all a game…, but for whom?

The Small Ferry: A Highlands and Islands Detective Thriller (Highlands & Islands Detective Book 4)
https://grjordan.com/product/the-small-ferry
A dreich day for a crossing and a small ferry packed to the gills. After off-loading one man sits dead at the wheel of the last remaining car. Can Macleod find the connections between the passengers, before the killer strikes again?

Macleod and McGrath return to Cromarty when a man is found dead at the wheel of his car on the local ferry. As the passengers are identified, the trail extends across the highlands and islands as past deeds are paid back in full. Can the seasoned pair hunt down a killer before their butchery spreads across the land?

When there's so much going on, it can be hard to see what's happening!

Surface Tensions (Island Adventures Book 1)

https://grjordan.com/product/surface-tensions

Mermaids sighted near a Scottish island. A town exploding in anger and distrust. And Donald's got to get the sexiest fish in town, back in the water.

"Surface Tensions" is the first story in a series of Island adventures from the pen of G R Jordan. If you love comic moments, cosy adventures and light fantasy action, then you'll love these tales with a twist.Get the book that amazon readers said, "perfectly captures life in the Scottish Hebrides" and that explores "human nature at its best and worst".

Something's stirring the water!

The Blasphemous Welcome: Dark Wen Book 1

https://grjordan.com/product/the-blasphemous-welcome

A demonic entity prepares a bloody path for its master. Four fiendish ways for the city folk to die. A cynical, battle weary detective must become his home's heavenly protector.

Join Detective Trimble and fresh faced Kyla Corstain as they enter a world of evil and ungodly manipulation causing murder, mayhem and disaster. The war for a city's soul begins now!

The Dark Wen series opens with a fanfare of destruction and death raining upon a city held in the grip of an unknown force. If you like dark powers, fast paced action and a generous dose of occult warfare, then "The Blasphemous Welcome" will satisfy your story cravings.

Lightning Source UK Ltd.
Milton Keynes UK
UKHW011415140121
376888UK00001B/4

9 781912 153947